I0760440

RISE OF THE WILD MOON

NEW WORLD SHIFTERS BOOK THREE

NINA WALKER

KIMBERLY LOTH

PROLOGUE

ELLE

The blood moon shines down over the carnage as if to mock us. I've seen a lot of gore in my life, but the scene before me is by far the worst. Death hangs heavy in the air, and the stench of it makes my stomach churn. The last shred of innocence I have left urges me to run away, but I can't. I have to face this. I'm with the Resistance so I knew this attack was coming, but I never expected it to be so ruthless--for so many to die.

The lycans are gone for now, having disappeared into the night, but they could return to finish off more wolves. They've taken out a good number of Ryne's pack, including some of the higher-ranked betas. Most of the claimed girls are huddled near the edge of the stage with tear-stained faces and glassy eyes. They're in shock. As a house mother, my duty is to go to them and offer comfort, but I can't right now.

I scan the scene for the people who are tied to my heart. My eyes first find Madame Delphine, and I sigh a breath of relief. The lycans know she's high in our ranks with the Resistance, but I can never be sure what they're going to do once they turn into monsters. Her hair is a mess, and her skirts are torn, but she's alive, and she's there, talking to the girls in a soft whisper. She'll take care of them. Not for the first time, I thank the heavens that she's my ally.

I spot my parents and brothers and nearly cry out in relief. They're walking among the dead and injured, checking for pulses and wrapping wounds. They should leave. It's not safe for them to be here anymore. I have no idea what the next few hours or days will bring, but if Thorn figures out that I was in on the plot for Poppy to marry Ryne, or that I knew this attack was coming, my parents' lives will be the first to go--after me, of course. As if my father can hear my thoughts, his eyes snap to mine.

"Go," I mouth, and he gives a stiff nod, taking my mother by the forearm and dragging her away. My brothers follow close behind. Father's actions appear rough, but that's always been a show for Thorn; my dad is one of the most gentle men I've ever met. He also probably knows that my mother won't leave me here, and he's hoping they'll be far enough away that they can't turn back when she realizes I've stayed behind.

I can't go with them. Even though my heart aches to leave, I have to stay. Our family can't afford any suspicion, and besides, I'll be alright. I'm the strongest female wolf who isn't already married off. Thorn will want me alive.

The stench of blood is thick in my nostrils as I walk through the wreckage, looking for those who I can help. I find my ripped dress and slip it back on. It barely stays put, and I consider dropping it altogether since I'm not shy about nudity, but I keep it on. It's something for me to fret about that isn't life or death, and as silly as that is, it calms me down a bit. In the back of my mind, I don't know how we'll recover from this, but in the forefront I can only deal with the here and now. I keep looking for Ryne, but he's nowhere to be found. It seems the alpha has disappeared, most likely with Poppy. I swallow a hard lump in my throat and try not to panic. That boy needs to come back immediately and take care of his pack. Otherwise his father will lose it. The king may even take control from his own son; he certainly threatened it earlier.

For now, the best I can do is damage control. There aren't many wounded left. They're all dead. The lycan were supposed to get Thorn! But this? They killed whoever they could. This wasn't the plan. I fist my hands and walk toward the far side of the stage--a place I don't want to be--where my enemies stand. Too bad I have to be the one to face them since all of my allies have fled.

Thorn stands tall, surveying the carnage with an angry frown. Of course the man is alive and well. What were the lycan thinking? Did they even try to attack him? Logically, I know they did, but I'm still mad as hell. Someone needs to get them in line, and if that person isn't going to be Madame Delphine, then it'll have to be me. They won't enjoy taking orders from a wolf, and a woman at that.

Thorn starts arguing with Anders, the angry tone in his voice rising above all the other noise. It's then that I finally take it in, as if my ears had gone deaf from sensory overload. Wolves howl all around us. Snarls and fights are still going on, but they are among each other, not the lycan. It's maddening that in a time like this, brothers can so easily turn on their own.

Ryne really needs to get back from wherever he ran off to; his pack needs him.

I put on my best smile and smooth my skirts. My heels are long gone, and I pad softly across the stage, my tattered wedding dress brushing around my ankles. I hold my head high and approach the two men. They're so enthralled with their argument they couldn't care less about me.

"You were supposed to kill him," Thorn hisses. "I gave you the chance, and you squandered it."

My blood runs cold when I realize they're talking about Ryne. Thorn really is okay with his only son dying, just to keep himself strong and in power. It goes to show how powerful Ryne is becoming if his father is afraid of him.

"I already told you the men wouldn't follow me if I did that," Anders whines.

"They wouldn't have had a choice, you idiot. You know what? I was wrong about you. You don't have the strength to lead this pack. I'll find another man."

I clear my throat, anger flaring to life. "I thought that man was Ryne, your *son*."

Thorn catches my eyes and an oily grin spreads across his lips like a stain. "Elle, love, why don't you go make sure our girls are okay? This must've been terribly traumatic for them. Go back to the house with them, and we'll come visit when we're done here."

I stand my ground. He's not going to get away with changing the subject. I know what I heard, and it makes me sick. "No. I'm a luna. I want to stay and help."

He raises an eyebrow. "Help with what? The lycan are gone, and the men are taking care of whatever comes next."

It takes everything in me not to spit at him for that comment. I'm so sick of being treated less-than because I'm a woman. "I'm just as capable as any man here, if not more so, and that includes Anders."

I can't help the dig, and Anders snorts in response.

If Thorn forces Ryne and me to marry, the first thing I will do is banish Anders. Now that he's challenged Ryne, I'm sure the others in the pack will be happy to see him leave. Sure, human wives don't have any say in what goes on in the pack. They are just pretty babymakers. But I've done some research. It turns out that before the wars, the luna wives would rule alongside their husbands as equals. In some cases, she even became the alpha.

If it happened before, it can happen again. There's a case to be made, and I plan to make it.

Thorn probably doesn't know any of this, or he would've killed me years ago. The man will do anything to preserve his power, and tonight proves it. Someday, someone will have enough power to overthrow him. That someone just may be me. Of course, if Ryne and I actually got married, there would be more of a chance of it happening. I'm not a fool though. There's no way I can stand between Ryne and his fated mate. Maybe someday I'll meet mine, assuming I even have one. I want that kind of love, but right now, love is most definitely not my priority. I eye Thorn, imagining him among the dead, and my resolve strengthens. I'd love to kill him right now, but I can't. I'd probably lose, and if I won, the pack would kill me, so I keep the fake smile on instead.

"You are likely right on that point. You are a capable young woman, aren't you?" Thorn chuckles, sliding closer to me. I nod, and my hackles rise. Something is off, but I can't quite put my finger on it. "Why don't you leave the tough stuff to the men? Even powerful lunas need their rest."

I stand a little taller. I'm not going anywhere. "I feel great, actually."

Something burns behind his eyes--a challenge? "When Ryne returns, the wedding will be performed, and you'll be in for a long night." He winks, and I have to resist the urge to punch him in the nose. "Actually, that might be a good job for you. Find Ryne and bring him back here."

I scoff. "You mean to tell me that you don't have dozens of wolves already out there looking for him?"

"I do. But according to you, you're better than they are."

"You're right, I am," I growl and move to the edge of the stage, ready to shift.

"On second thought, why don't you wait on that," Thorn calls after me, and I spin around to face him. He studies me with curious eyes and approaches. He stands way too close. His chest is bare, and blood oozes from a wound across his collarbone. His nostrils flare with every breath as he stares at me for way too long. He brings a hand up to my face and forces me to look him in the eye. I stare at him defiantly.

"You are right. You are the most powerful wolf here. You will make Ryne a very strong alpha."

I nod stiffly, his fingers still digging into my chin.

He purses his lips. "Perhaps I do not want him to be a stronger alpha anymore. You saw how he disappointed me tonight. He doesn't deserve a fine specimen such as yourself."

What is he saying?

"If you pass me on to Anders . . ." I let the unsaid threat hang in the air. I don't know what I would do, but Anders would die before he touched me.

Thorn chuckles. "I'm not going to pass you on to Anders. He's proven he's a weak wolf as well. No. I've come to a realization tonight. Can you guess what it is?" He doesn't wait for my answer. "If you want something done right, you have to do it yourself."

Dread fills my stomach, and I hope he's not saying what I think he's saying. "I don't understand." The words feel like sand in my mouth.

"Oh, I think you do. You will be married tonight, but Ryne won't be your new husband." His eyes flash with desire and greed, and he steals me into his arms. "I will."

CHAPTER 1

I don't even have shoes. And while there are a lot of things I could probably do without here in the wilds, shoes are not one of them. About an hour into walking on my bare feet, I rip off part of my ruined slip and tie the fabric around my injured soles, but it offers little protection, and I'm still slowing us down. The blood at my ankle has stopped flowing, but two crescent moon bite marks throb next to the bone. I'm desperate to sit and rest for a while, but I can't.

I'm not even sure where we're going. Knox and I have been walking through the darkness along the edge of an abandoned road. It's overgrown with weeds, and the concrete is broken up in parts, but at least it's a landmark to go by. He doesn't want to stop, saying we need to get as far away from the city as we can, but it's grown darker, and even though the full moon brightens the landscape, it's not nearly enough light to continue by for much longer.

"I think the adrenaline has worn off," I say, my voice

coming out achingly hoarse. Maybe from screaming, maybe from the lycan venom. I don't know.

"Yeah, me too," he sighs.

"We need to set up a camp."

"What camp? We don't have any equipment, and besides, walking is the smartest move right now."

I'm not so sure that's true.

"Where are we even going?" I've been afraid to ask because I've been scared of the answer.

"West, I guess," he says despondently. "We're banished. Think I don't know what happens to banished people?" He points to the moon and shivers. "They die."

"Or they get bitten." I lift up my ankle. "At least I have another full month to figure something out before I end up turning into a monster."

Even though he winces at my bluntness, I can't pretend it didn't happen. I'm a walking time bomb. A less selfish person would tell Knox to get away from me, maybe even help him find a better life. I am not that person. The truth is that being alone out here is terrifying, and as twisted as it is, I'm grateful that Knox is with me.

"I have an idea." He points into the distance. "One of the villages is just over those hills. I'm going to sneak in there and find us food, clothing, and maybe some boots for you." I wouldn't blame him if he just stayed in the village and left me here. It's his safest option.

"That's stealing," I argue. He gives me an annoyed look. Even in the moonlight, I can tell he's frustrated. "Okay, fair enough," I quickly relent, "but I'm not letting you go alone."

"Pretty sure you're less than conspicuous in that outfit."

"I guess you have a point." I stop in my tracks, glaring

down at the ruined slip and what remains of the ugly bodice. "Wait, no, you can't go tonight. You'll have to go tomorrow."

"Plan is to be long gone by tomorrow."

"But wolf shifters guard the settlements on full moons."

He gives me a sad look. "When are you going to realize that most of what you were told was a lie? How many wolves did you see protecting our village when we were growing up?"

I swallow hard. "None, but that doesn't mean they weren't farther out."

"The wolves are far more concerned with protecting their city than they ever were with the villages. Trust me, I'll be fine."

I wonder for a moment how we managed to stay safe on the full moons. The villages would be easy pickings for the lycan. It makes no sense that the wolves would leave them vulnerable to attack, but I can see his point too. I don't remember seeing wolves on full moons, and the stories about the lycans were mostly just that. Stories.

I end up sitting against a thin tree trunk, hidden inside a little grove of aspen, as Knox goes off to play hero or abandon me completely. I vow to stay awake as I wait for him to get back, and for a long time I do, but eventually exhaustion overwhelms me, and I give up the fight.

Hours later? Minutes? Urgent hands shake me. My automatic reflex is to scream, but Knox is quick to palm my mouth. Once I'm aware of what's going on, he carefully removes his hand. It's sweaty--he's been running. Gratitude surges in my chest. He came back.

"Did you get anything?" I whisper, eager for those

boots.

"No." His breath comes out ragged. "But we have to go. Now."

He drags me up, and we run into the nearby forest. No road. No path. Just underbrush to slice at my legs and rip my dress even further. My eyes have adjusted better to the darkness, but that advantage is short-lived once the trees grow thicker. It won't be long until one of us rolls an ankle or worse.

"Slow down," I gasp. I'm a runner, but this is madness.

He whirls on me, pushing one hand against my mouth again and holding his index finger up to his lips in a shushing motion.

That's when I hear the howls.

The adrenaline rushes back. If it's lycan, we're probably dead. If it's wolves, we may stand a chance, but that's only assuming word hasn't traveled. I'm a fugitive now. What I did to King Thorn won't be forgotten. All I can hope for is that the king believes me dead. That's not going to happen if someone reports back about seeing us out here. Thorn will follow my scent, and I'll be a goner by morning.

Knox leans close, mouth pressed against my ear. "We can't be found."

Now it's my turn for an idea. I point up. He doesn't seem to understand, and I'm too scared to say anything aloud, so I begin to climb. Up and up I go. The pine needles are scratchy and sticky, and the bark catches on everything, but the higher I climb, the safer I feel. Knox follows and is soon only an arm's length below me. Eventually, I find a large bare branch and relax onto it, my back against the trunk. Knox stops at one a few feet down and does the same. The pine has thinned enough up here that we can see the whole valley. I don't know if it will make a difference.

My mind races back to everything that transpired tonight. I made a gamble and nearly won, but the lycans showed up and ruined everything. At least I got Joanna and Grady out of there alive. Thorn was going to kill them, and I just hope Grady is okay. He lost his arm, and he might bleed out, leaving Joanna vulnerable. She's part of the Resistance though. She's got contacts and people who can help her. She'll be okay so long as she doesn't have to face Thorn ever again. The man is a monster. It's hard to believe that he had Anders challenge Ryne, and it proves he's far crueler than I ever thought possible. If he knew I was bitten and currently on the run, I'd be hunted down to the bitter end and made to suffer. I stood up to the man, and nobody does that. Even Ryne has a hard time with it. I just hope Ryne is able to convince him I died. A lump forms in my throat at the thought of my fated mate. I recall the look of sheer panic on his face when he saw I'd been bit, and my heart squeezes.

But then I remember that he was going to let our friends die. How could he think I'd marry him right after their executions? And now that we've parted ways, I don't think I'll ever understand his reasoning. He put his father before them, and it's unforgivable. I'll probably never see him again, and maybe that's okay, because he isn't the man I thought he was. Tears threaten, but I hold them in, focusing on the darkened forest below instead, listening and waiting.

Knox and I sit like this for ages. This time, I don't fall asleep.

CHAPTER 2

The sun peeks over the trees. Knox still sits one branch below me, his head bobbing. I understand the feeling, but if we fall asleep up here, we could plunge to our deaths. I reach down and tap him on the head. He jerks around and blinks up at me. Do I look as tired and wild as he does? His buzzed blonde hair has broken leaves and thistles stuck to it, and his face is covered in dirt and scratches.

"Is it safe?" I mouth.

He swallows and glances around. "I think so." His voice is barely above a whisper. He slowly makes his way down the tree, and I follow. We both land on the ground with a soft thud, and I nearly cry out. My feet will not survive this trip because my poor ankle is thrashed. Tears spring to my eyes because I suddenly don't know what to do. We're going to get killed because of me, and if we somehow make it out of here, I'm still going to become a lycan on the next full moon. My life is over.

"Are you okay?" Knox is obviously concerned, and I can't lie to him about this. He needs to know what he's signing up for.

I shake my head and point at the wounds.

When Knox kneels down to study them, worry settles over his features. "We'll have to fix that problem today. But first, we need to find a place to get some sleep, water, and food if we can. I don't know where we are now, but we'll figure it out."

I'm a coward because I don't say anything. If I was brave, I would insist he ditch me to save himself. Instead, we walk for what feels like hours, but is probably only thirty minutes. Each step is agony, and I don't know how much more I can take. I always thought I was strong and capable, but obviously I overestimated my abilities.

The ground becomes soft and squishy. I glance down. My feet are covered in water. It's freezing cold and brings sweet relief.

"I think we found water," I point out, smiling to myself. I think it's the first time I've smiled in what feels like ages.

Knox only nods, but I don't mind because neither one of us has the energy to talk much. After a few minutes of letting me numb my ankle, he glances around with a determined look on his face. "Stay there for a minute, and I'll see if I can find a place to rest."

I shift a little so I can lean against a tree, but I leave both feet in the water. I know it's probably going to open them up to all kinds of infection, but at the moment, I don't care. If I can get the swelling down, maybe I can go on a little longer.

After several minutes, Knox returns. His brown eyes

sparkle, and I know he's found what he was looking for. "This turns into a stream not too far that way." He motions over his shoulder. "There's several trees and soft ground where we can get some rest and then figure out what to do next."

I follow him in a daze. Something scratches my arm, and I glance down. It's a bush with bright black berries. "Knox, stop." He turns and spots the berries as well.

"Do you think they're safe?"

He nods. "We had these at home. Blackberries are fine. Good catch, Poppy."

I don't hesitate to pluck several off and shove them in my mouth. The sweet and tart juice is heavenly. I glance at Knox. He's doing the same, and when he smiles at me, his teeth are stained purple. I laugh because mine probably are too.

We don't eat too many because even in our delirium, we know that it could make us sick. The area Knox found is indeed a comfortable-looking spot. We drink from the stream. Knox says it's fine since we know it comes out of the ground where we just were, and I don't think I've ever been more grateful for water. Once sated, we settle against a large tree with springy moss along the bottom. My body relaxes right away, and my feet don't hurt as bad.

"Do you think one of us should stay awake in case we're attacked?" I ask.

He chuckles, trying to hold off a yawn and failing. "Could we fight them off anyway in this state?"

"Good point."

My eyes flutter closed, and before I know it, sleep claims me.

I don't know where I'm going, and I'm certain it will be horrible, but at least I don't have to walk anymore.

"Are you going to kill me?" I ask the man.

"If you give me a reason to," he responds. "Now be quiet, or else I'll bind your mouth too."

I hate being afraid, hate the way my muscles tense and my heart speeds. I hate how my thoughts become muddled and frantic all at once. I've been in fight-or-flight mode for months, and I don't know if I can handle another second of it. I try to relax, to force the panic back, but it proves impossible. I don't know who these men and women are, but one thing I've learned about people lately is that they can't be trusted.

Not even Ryne. Not even my fated mate.

Blood rushes to my head because this mountain of a man has me tossed over his shoulder like a sack of potatoes. I try to lift my neck up but can't hold the position for long, so I end up with my head resting against his bare back. It's hot today, and his sweat sticks to my cheek. I breathe through my mouth to try and lessen his stench--he clearly hasn't bathed in a while.

Knox is forced to walk, probably because he doesn't have any injuries. He's a few paces behind us, arms tied behind his back, with guards on either side. His eyes hold mine as he mouths, "it's going to be okay."

It's a lie and an attempt to coddle me, maybe even his way to love me right now. Make me believe life can't possibly get worse, force me to think about other things. He used to do the same when we were dating, and I'd worry about his claiming. I don't need that kind of love anymore. I don't need love at all actually. I need loyalty, and I need the truth.

I look away and study the rest of the group. It's hard to count them in this position, but I'd guess there are about twenty people here. There are more men than women, but not by much. The women seem just as scary and weathered as the men do. They're nothing like the women back in the city who are constantly dressed up like dollies to be played with.

As we continue, a headache starts to build. Just when I think my brain is going to combust, the man sets me down. "I'm going to put a blindfold on you now," he says, dropping his gaze to mine. He's about my father's age, and it makes me miss the days when I could trust the adults in my life, especially the men. "If you fight me, I'll knock you out."

I see no point in fighting him. I'm too weak.

I nod wearily as a strip of fabric is tied over my eyes. I can see specs of light coming from around my nose, but it's not enough to make a difference. We must be getting close to wherever their camp is, and they don't want us to know the exact location. I want to tell him that it's pointless and that I don't know where I am anyway, but I don't. I'd like to keep all my teeth.

Even though I can't see it, I can tell my ankle has swelled up even more. It tingles and throbs like crazy, and when I try to take a step forward, I can't. I wince and fall to my knees. A few people chuckle, but not everyone. Maybe there will be someone here who is sympathetic to me, who will help me. More than likely I'll end up dead, but I can't allow my mind to think about that right now. I want to survive but I'm injured and facing the very real possibility that this could be the end for me. I'm starting to lose all fight.

Luckily, the man picks me back up and carries me again. I'll gladly take his sweat and stench over walking on this ankle. We continue on for another twenty minutes or so, and then we climb into something. From the way we rock gently and the sound of lapping water, I know we're in a boat. I expect an engine to rumble to life, but it doesn't. Maybe they don't have fuel? Someone must be rowing.

Only a few short minutes later, we hit a shoreline, and I'm carried off the boat.

So we crossed the river--I file that information away, just in case.

We're back to walking, but branches brush against us this time. We're definitely moving through some kind of well-hidden path, probably going deeper into the forest. If I were these people and had to figure out a way to survive out here, I'd do the same. I keep thinking we're going to stop, but we just keep going and going. With the blindfold on and the blood pooling in my head, I grow disoriented. Eventually, I fall asleep.

Thump! I wake up with a start as I'm dropped to the ground. I expect the pain of hard earth, but there's none. The blindfold is gone. And so are the people and Knox. All that's left is me and this burly man. But I'm not on the ground, am I? I gasp and crawl back, fear pulsing through my body. This is a tent. I'm on thick rugs, and we're all alone in here.

Is this it then? Is he going to take my virtue?

"We're not the wolves." He sneers, leering over me,

obviously sensing my fear. "We don't take women to our beds against their will."

I let out a breath.

"But we don't tolerate liars, thieves, or spies either." He looks me in the eye. His are brown and ringed in yellow. "I won't hesitate to kill you if need be."

Why hasn't he already? He knows I've been bit.

And that's when it hits me. The way they smell, why they were close to the city, why they seem to hate the wolves, and most of all, why they didn't kill me the second they found my bite wound. These aren't ordinary humans.

They're lycan.

CHAPTER 3

"I'm not a spy. If you just let me and my friend go, we won't bother you again."

The man snorts and rocks back on his haunches. "We're not letting you go. You've been bitten. You're going to need our help."

I bristle a little bit. I don't want help from a man like this. I don't want help at all. I never want to go through my first shift because I don't want to be a lycan.

"You can't help me. I won't attack people." Even as I say it, my throat hollows.

He chuckles. "Oh yes, you will, and you'll like it, but that's a discussion for another day. Today, you will tell me who you are and where you came from. Keep in mind that my mate is asking your friend the same questions, and if your answers are different, even just a little bit, both of you will die. We will not risk our people."

I swallow. Knox and I didn't talk about this at all. I have no idea what answers Knox is giving, and the only chance we have at getting things right is to answer honestly. I'll just keep my answers as short as possible and hope for mercy.

"Fine. My real name is Poppy, and we came from the wolf city."

The man stands and paces, his brow furrowed in thought. "Are you from the mating houses, a beta wife, or one of the claimed?"

"The claimed."

"So you must have been in the city during the festival and got bitten in the raid. How did you get to the wilds before a wolf found and killed you?"

This is the part that I am unsure of how Knox will answer. I don't want to use Ryne's name if I can avoid it. I hesitate for a moment.

"Answer me," the man screams in my face.

"Knox was a driver--one of the claimed men. He got us out."

"And why would he help you?"

"Because we are from the same village, and we were . . . friends before the claiming."

The man's lips twitch. "Friends, huh? I won't kill you for that omission. Now, tell me, Poppy, why does that bodice look suspiciously like the top of a torn wedding dress? The wolves don't take wives until the harvest."

Once again, I hope Knox goes with a half-truth here as well. "One of the betas took a liking to me and asked for my hand early. The alpha agreed."

"Which beta?"

I wonder for a moment how much this man knows. If he's asking for specific names, then he must know the city.

Maybe he was one of the lycan that came in and attacked. From the scratches all over him, I wouldn't be surprised.

"Nico," I say.

He stands and paces again.

"Will Nico come after you?"

"I don't know, but I doubt it. I'm not his fated mate or anything like that."

"If he loved you so much that he convinced the alpha to move up the wedding date, then why wouldn't he come after you?"

I swallow, thinking of how I can spin this. Going with half-truths seems like the best course of action. I look the man dead in the eyes and strengthen my resolve. I will not die today. "Nico knew I was bitten when I left with Knox."

"He should've killed you." He stops and stares at me, curiosity alight in his eyes.

"He should've, but he didn't."

The man cocks his head. "Hmm, that's interesting. A wolf who let his little lycan go? How romantic." He scoffs. "You're not telling me everything, but you've told me enough to keep you alive. Count yourself lucky."

He turns on his heel and exits the tent. I hang my head between my knees. My hands are still tied up behind my back, and my ankles are bound together once more. I can hardly move, and everything hurts. Now that the man is gone and my adrenaline has slowed, I can feel every ache and pain. But underneath it all is something else--a burning in my veins. I know what it is, but I can't face it yet. Instead, I focus on the man and what he could be doing next. He said I'll get to live, but he seemed quite interested in my relationship with Nico. Could he be planning to use me against the wolves?

Ugh, probably. Maybe I shouldn't have said so much.

Now that he's gone, I figure he's going to find out if Knox and I gave the same answers. If we didn't, we might die. If we did, I'll live for the time being, but I'm not sure about Knox. I don't really want to hang out with a bunch of lycan, especially if they end up killing Knox, but I don't see that I have any other choice. Maybe if I can get them to trust me, Knox and I can figure out how to run away.

I feel better now that I have a plan.

The tent flap rustles, and I tense. This time a woman enters. She's nearly as tall as the man, wearing a worn tank top and baggy pants that have a couple of holes. Her boots stomp hard on the ground, and she holds a wicked-looking knife.

There is a long scar across her face, and when she smiles at me, I notice she's missing three teeth. She lunges for me, and I jump.

She cackles up a storm.

"You should see your face. So scared."

"You're holding a knife."

She crouches in front of me, her putrid breath assaulting my nostrils. Do these people not bathe, or are they smelly because they've recently spent the night as lycans? She holds up the knife. "And I want nothing more than to carve your skin right off your body, but Laik said your stories check out, so I have to let you go. But I come with a warning."

I swallow and nod. The brutish man who carried me must be Laik.

"We have three rules in camp. One, you do your chores even if you don't like them. Two, no fighting. Three, you listen to Laik and do whatever he says without question, which is why I'm letting you go instead of cutting you up. But for you, there is a fourth rule."

"Okay." The rules seem somewhat reasonable. Though number three concerns me.

"You and your friend are not allowed to talk or interact in any way. If you accidentally make eye contact, you look away immediately. I'll be watching you, and if you fail to follow this rule, I have full permission to use this knife on you."

"For how long?" I gasp. This rule is just cruel. Knox is the only person I have left.

"Until Laik says. You should pretend your friend doesn't exist."

Running away is impossible now. If Knox and I can't even talk, we'll never be able to make any plans, and I won't leave without him. He stuck by me, and I'm going to stick by him. Rule number four can't last forever though, and when we no longer have it, we'll figure out how to get out of here. We'll live on our own or in a human village that can take us in. I will not stay with these monsters. And when it comes time for me to turn, I'll lock myself up somewhere I can't hurt anybody. It's not ideal, but I can make it work.

The woman takes the knife and slices the ropes free from my legs, then she moves behind me, nicking my wrists with the blade.

"Oops," she says with a giggle. "Better get you to medical."

I manage to climb to my feet, but I'm still limping quite a bit. I was right that my ankle swelled up. It looks like a damn balloon.

"What's your name?" I ask her while trying to hold back a sob.

"Didn't I say? I'm Wanda." Her eyes go glassy. "Wanda will be watching Poppy." She opens the tent flap, and I step out into the blinding sun. All around me people bustle about, and panic sets in. In my haste to get away from Wanda, I forgot where I am and who I'm with.

Lycan...

At least, I think they're lycan. There are about thirty of them here and they look like humans, but they're rough around the edges. Probably from living like this. The camp is made up of camouflaged tents sitting among tall pines. A babbling brook winds through it, where many of the people are washing up in various states of undress. So maybe they smelled bad because they weren't here on the full moon. Laik is among them. He's a beast of a man and completely naked.

I avert my eyes, and my cheeks warm.

"Does she think she's better than us?" someone says gruffly. "She won't be one to talk come next month."

"Go easy on her," a woman's voice cuts through. I want to look, but I keep my head down. I don't want these people to notice me, let alone think I'm watching them bathe. "Laik says she was one of the claimed girls. Don't you think she's been through enough?"

"I know she's a liar," someone bounces back.

"That's enough." Laik's voice cuts them off, and I look up. I meet his eyes, careful to avoid the rest of him. "Our lycan self has a distinct stench that hangs around until we can wash it away. And Chase is right. You will be one of us soon." He nods toward a tent. "Now, go see Callum and get yourself patched up. There's no downtime here."

I wobble over to the tent. The flap is already open with the scent of sandalwood drifting out. "Come in," a young male voice says. I don't know what I was expecting of the healer, but I assumed elderly and probably female. The last thing I want to do is go into a tent with a male, but I have to take Laik's word for it. Nobody is going to touch me against my will here.

I duck inside to find a cramped space with a couple cots, blankets, and a table covered in dried herbs. The man inside can hardly be called a man. He's got to be younger than I am. "I already know what you're thinking," he says, "I was the apprentice for three months when our medicine woman died, so here I am. Have a seat."

Settling onto a flat pillow, I try not to wince. The swelling has started to go down, but somehow that's made it worse. It's like the ligaments have loosened too much. The boy kneels before me and begins examining the ankle. "Doesn't look infected," he says. "You're lucky. A third of the bites are, and not everyone can survive an infection out here. We don't always have access to antibiotics, you know."

I swallow hard. "How do I know if it's infected?" I don't even get to the part about antibiotics. I don't know what they are, and I feel out of touch enough as it is.

He sighs, and I take the opportunity to get a better look at him. If I had to guess, I'd put him no older than seventeen. He's got edgy features and long black hair tied into a messy bun. He doesn't look like anyone from my village, but he does remind me of the men back in the wolf pack. It makes me miss Ryne, and I squash down that longing immediately. Ryne betrayed Grady and Joanna and then sent me off to die. If he really cared about me, he wouldn't have fed me to the lycan--he knows who lives out in the wilds. But then again, should I be surprised? He was going to kill our friends, all to please his father. When things get tough, it turns out Ryne chooses Thorn.

"The edges will turn red, it will start to pus, and you'll get a fever. So watch for those things. You'll need to keep it clean. Good thing is, after your first renewal, you'll be able to heal from wounds quickly."

"Renewal?"

"That's what we call it when we shift," he explains. "With each moon we become stronger than the last."

"But that doesn't really explain 'renewal.'"

He pauses for a second. "Listen, you didn't hear this from me, but you'll learn soon enough anyway, so I may as well be the first to explain it to you." He leans forward and smiles conspiratorially. He doesn't smell like the others, and his breath is fine. He must have already bathed. "We can only change into our lycan forms during full moons, but we do have extra strengths during the month. The new moon, when there is nothing in the sky, is when we're at our weakest."

"What kind of strengths?"

He shrugs a shoulder like it's nothing, but I realize he's bragging, and his eyes keep flashing to my bare legs. I hate that I'm still in this torn slip, but Callum's checking me out, which could play to my advantage.

"We're fast and strong, and we can heal quickly. It's nothing like when we're lycan, but we're still better than humans." He holds up a hand. "No offense."

"None taken." But that's not true. I am kind of offended. I don't want to become one of these brutal monsters that kill humans, and now that I know they think they're better than humans, I like them even less.

"I'm Callum, by the way," he reaches out a weathered hand, and we shake.

Over the next few minutes, I ask him questions while he packs and binds my wound, but I don't learn anything else new. He also treats the cuts on my feet, rubbing goo into them and covering them in bandages. He hands over some slippers and tells me where I can find a set of clean clothes in another tent. On my way out, he gives me some herbs to take for the next few weeks. "Some will help you get rid of the inflammation and pain, and others will prepare your body for your renewal next month."

"Which ones work for which things?" I ask curiously.

He seems excited that I'm interested and spends the next five minutes going through each one. I listen intently and then thank him as I leave. Even though part of me knows I shouldn't, I decide I'm not going to use any of the herbs meant to help me through the renewal. I'll take the stuff for my wounds, but that's it. Maybe it's stupid, but I can't help but wonder if the lycan are wrong about me. What if I'm stronger than all of this? Maybe I'll get lucky, and my body will fight off the lycan venom on its own. If taking Callum's herbs will help me turn into a lycan, then I'm going to do the exact opposite.

CHAPTER 4

By lunchtime, the offensive stench of the lycan is washed away. Everyone has bathed and is wearing fresh clothes. They look a million times more put together than they did when I first met them. I catch sight of Knox every once in a while, but I avoid his eyes, and I notice that he avoids mine. I worry that they might change him on purpose. He's in far more danger than I am in this camp. Eventually we'll figure out how to talk to one another, but for now, I must keep my head down and let myself heal. At least, the bits of me that can heal. It's not just my ankle that's torn to shreds. It's my heart too, and I don't think that'll ever be the same.

I wear thick socks, boots, cargo pants, and a tight tank top. Most of the other women are dressed similarly, though they wear sandals or tennis shoes. It's getting warmer, and summer is fast approaching. The humidity will be brutal out here in the wilds, but at least my feet will be better by then. The woman who gave me clothes told me they needed time to heal and to keep them in socks until they do. I'd tried to strike up a conversation with her, but the mention of socks was all she offered. It was apparent she didn't want to talk, and I know she won't be the only one here who wants to steer clear of me. I'm the outsider, and Laik already told them I came from the wolf city. They don't trust me, and I can't say I blame them. I wouldn't trust me either if I was in their position.

After changing, I wander around the camp. I'm not really sure what to do. A few people introduce themselves, but most just go on ignoring me. They won't even share eye contact. I don't take offense or try to push them. I need to focus on staying alive, and Mama always said you catch more bees with honey than vinegar. It may kill me to keep my tongue in check while I'm here, but it may also save me.

The camp is set up in a circle. There are folding tables and an outdoor kitchen at the center surrounded by large canvas tents that groups of people sleep in. The biggest ones are for men and women, but there are a few for couples, and Laik has his own. The supply tents, medic's tent, and the tent Laik questioned me in form an outer circle. I don't go into any of the tents, but I watch as people go in and come out with supplies--food, clothes, and even a few weapons.

I don't know what to do with myself, so I sit to the side and watch, my aching feet starting to ease up a little. I think Callum's herbs are starting to work, and it sends a wave of relief through me. He's not so bad. I'm still not going to touch the ones he gave me to prepare for the next full moon, but I'm definitely sticking with the healing herbs.

Lunch rolls around, and it doesn't smell like much, but hunger has turned my stomach raw, and I need to fill it up. I walk on shaky legs and go to the line. I stand with the rest of them and get a gooey brown mush along with a roll dumped onto a metal plate. I sit at the farthest table and pick at the food. The mush looks off, and I can't even tell what's in it. My stomach turns in protest. Maybe I'm not as hungry as I thought.

"It tastes better than it looks," Callum says with a chuckle. I jerk my eyes up, and he sits next to me. He's the first person to actually look me in the eyes in hours, and I'm instantly grateful. Maybe we can be friends.

"What is it?" I ask, almost afraid of the answer.

He shrugs. "A mix of grains, vegetables, and legumes. See, there's a carrot." He points to a pale orange lump. "We add deer meat when we can get it, but there's not any in there today. All vegetarian, baby." He winks, and I think it's rather ironic that a bunch of lycans aren't eating meat. Callum's trying to lighten the mood, so I give him a small smile before returning to stare at the supposedly edible sludge. I sniff at it, take a small bite, and grimace. It does not taste better than it looks.

"Oh look, the princess thinks she's better than our food." Wanda takes the seat next to me and looks me up and down with a curled lip.

"I'm no princess," I grumble.

Callum hands me a salt shaker. "Use as much as you need."

I practically dump the whole thing on my food and choke it down. At least the roll tastes alright. Hopefully my stomach will thank me, but I'm not so sure. This is a far cry from the meals we had at the manor. Even the villages eat better than this.

"At dinner we get berries and things for dessert," he adds hopefully. "It's my favorite meal of the day."

"Is it all like this?" I ask. My voice comes out whiny, and I instantly regret the question.

"Yes," Wanda grunts. "You should be grateful you aren't starving, little girl. We don't have to feed you, let alone keep you safe. You're lucky Laik is willing to help." It's obvious she'd taken a different route if she was the leader here. The woman hates me.

But she's also right. It's not that I want to stay here with the lycan, but I can't turn my nose up at them either. And I guess it makes sense now that nobody wants to go to the wilds because they're, well, *wild.* What else are people supposed to eat out here?

"You're right. I'm sorry. I'm just not used to it."

She sniffs. "We eat for fuel here, so finish that because you're going to need the energy."

I force another mouthful and nod. Again, she's right, even if I don't like it.

"I know the wolves gotta keep their babymakers well-fed in the city." She eyes my stomach. "You aren't pregnant with one of those monsters, are you?"

Monsters? The lycan are also monsters. I've made the argument myself that the wolves are monsters too, so I guess I can see where she's coming from. But not all of them. My heart clenches. I miss Ryne more than anything and hate that I care so much about him.

"I'm not pregnant," I mutter. "Promise."

She shrugs. "Wouldn't matter anyway. You'll be a lycan

soon, and the change from human to lycan wouldn't let you keep a baby anyway."

My mouth pops open. "So I'll never have children?" It's not like I want to bring a child into this world, because I certainly don't, but the idea that I'll become infertile if I turn is jarring.

"No," Callum cuts in, shooting Wanda a stern look. "Sometimes lycan women have children, but a pregnant human has never had a baby survive the first renewal. It's too hard on the body. Anyway, you won't get your chore assignments until tomorrow morning, but I was wondering if you wanna come help me sort herbs and fold dressing?" His cheeks pink slightly, and his eyes are so hopeful that I don't know how to answer.

"Poppy is coming with me," Laik's strong voice carries across from the next table over where he sits near Knox. I turn towards him and offer a thumbs up. He takes that as confirmation and returns to shoveling food into his mouth. I don't know what Laik wants with me, but whatever it is, it's not going to be nearly as pleasant as spending the afternoon with Callum, even if the boy is a little too eager.

We finish up, and I follow the others to drop my scraped-clean plate into a vat of soapy water. I ate it all, even though it tasted awful, because Wanda made a good point and also because I don't want to make anyone hate me more than they already do. The dishes reek, and I eye the water with a grimace. I really hope that I'm not assigned dish duty tomorrow.

I can't even begin to think about what it's like to eat this way day in and day out. I hope I'm not here for long.

CHAPTER 5

I search the group of people cleaning up and find Laik standing near the path to the forest. I approach him cautiously. Instead of saying a word to me, he grabs the handle of a wagon and tromps down the path. I have to hurry to keep up with the man. He's huge, almost as tall as Ryne, and much bulkier. I wince a little as my feet still hurt, but the boots are keeping them safe from new wounds, so I can't complain.

"Where are we going?"

"To gather wood for the dinner fire." He pulls a long saw out of the wagon. "I'll get some of the bigger pieces if you'll gather kindling."

Okay, that's not so bad.

I search the ground for small branches, and he cuts up bigger ones. We work in silence for a long time, and it's actually peaceful. If this is my job, I'll gladly scour the woods with Laik. He doesn't scare me as much as his mate does. At least, I assume that Wanda is his mate. She certainly seems possessive of him. I hope I'm right, that he isn't so bad, but a little voice in the back of my head is warning me to be careful.

"Do we get new chores every day, or is it the same?" I ask.

Laik dumps a few logs into the wagon and brushes his hands on his pants. "It depends on the job and the day. More specialized jobs, like medical, are the same every day, but things like gathering wood and dishes are rotated around. You'll be doing a little of everything to see if you have talents in any particular area. Is there anything you're good at?"

I recall my time at Drayton Hall. I learned a thing or two, but not well. The only thing I excelled at was running and fighting. I'm not sure I want to fight for the lycan, but it would get me out a little more. The people who guard the camp get to roam the outskirts, and most of them have weapons. I could use that to my advantage and get out of here.

"I'm a pretty good fighter."

Laik eyes me up and down. "You're too small to fight."

I hold my head high. "I assure you I can hold my own. I know you have patrols and guards. Let me be one of them."

He laughs, and I'm surprised by the joyfulness of the sound. He doesn't strike me as the kind of guy to take a joke. "We will see if you can fight, though I doubt you're any good. Either way, you aren't joining our guard until you prove your loyalty to me."

Oh, so he was laughing *at* me. I sniff. Fat chance of that. I'll never be loyal to them. But I don't want to be on kitchen duty the rest of my time here, either. I'll never escape that way. Considering my other training at the manor, I could try to get this guy to like me. I'm not about to flirt with him, but if he sees me as one of his own, I'll get what I want faster. "What do I have to do to prove my loyalty?"

He stares at me, scrutinizing my every word and action. Something changes between us, and I can't tell if it's more trust or less trust, but whatever it is, the man is starting to see me as more than a silly girl who ate his berries. "You're serious, aren't you?"

"I am. I have no love for the wolves who forced me from my home and then abandoned me when I got hurt." It's a half-lie. They did do all those things, but I still love Ryne. Perhaps that's the curse of being his fated mate. I'm doomed to love a man I should hate, a man I'll never trust again or see again or…

I can't think about that.

Laik nods slowly, and a muscle pops in his jaw. "Okay, give us some time, and we'll see what we can come up with. Give yourself time as well. Adjusting to being a lycan isn't easy. We can resume this conversation after your first renewal."

I swallow. I'd forgotten that I'm one of them. I don't have time for my renewal to swing around. I need to get out of here and find a cure to this curse before it takes me hostage for good. Everything has already changed in my life, but if I become a lycan, there will be no going back. Not ever.

* * *

Dinner is better than lunch but not by much. The food is bland again, and I don't have an appetite. I keep thinking about what Laik said about adjusting to being a lycan. It's only been a few hours, but the idea of a cure suddenly seems like a foolish fantasy. I've never heard of one before, and that's because there isn't one. Maybe I should take Callum's herbs, after all? I don't know what to do.

The thoughts weigh heavy on my mind, and I have a nagging feeling that there's a lot more to becoming a lycan. When Charlotte turned, she killed a bunch of people. What if that happens to me too? I don't know if I'll be able to forgive myself. I want to run away, but that could be a mistake. Maybe if I stay and have my first renewal with these people, they can help me, and once I have a better idea of what I can and cannot handle, I can make a run for it. Is that a terrible idea? Should I get out of here before it becomes impossible to leave? I don't want to go through my first shift on my own, but I don't want to trust these people either.

It's an impossible situation and has hit me like a slap to the face. I've been in denial the last few days, but I can't deny it anymore. I've been infected, and I'm going to turn into a monster.

"What's going on with the alpha?" a woman asks a man as he settles in for his meal. They're not talking to me, but I listen intently while keeping my eyes down. I don't want them to know I'm eavesdropping on them. The guy she's talking to is burly and still reeks like a beast and is covered in dirt. He must have just arrived back at camp. He surveys the group, eyes landing on me and holding. I don't meet his gaze, but I can feel it lingering on me like a shadow.

I grow hot, fear washing through me. Was he at the festival? Did he see me? Does he know about me and Ryne? If anyone here finds out I'm fated to Ryne, that knowledge will be used against me. Either that, or I'll simply be murdered for my association with their enemy.

The man looks away. "Not sure what you're talking about," he responds.

The woman gives the man a look. "Everyone knows what you were doing there. Is the alpha married or not?"

My breath catches. So then that man *was* there that night. He probably saw me and is going to tell everyone. I'll go from being the lost berry-girl to the enemy's fated mate. For the first time all day, I catch Knox's eye. He sits on the far side of another table, and he's looking at me too. He shakes his head once and returns to his plate. His ears are pink. Is he afraid? For him or for me?

Now everyone within earshot is watching him. He takes a bite of his bread and slowly chews, leaving us suspended. I feel as if I'm two seconds from exploding. Because it's an answer I need to know as well. Is the alpha married? Surely after everything, the weddings didn't happen.

The man swallows, takes a long drink from his cup, and sighs with satisfaction.

"Enough with the theatrics, Tanner." Laik sits right next to me, and I can feel the tension rolling off of his body.

Wanda slams the table with her fist and yells, "Tell us!" For once, I agree with her.

"Sorry, sorry." Tanner laughs, eyeing the whole table. "I didn't realize y'all were so eager to know." He prolongs the suspense for a few moments longer. No one is eating anymore, and every eye is on him. "Yes, despite everything, the alpha got married to the luna."

Laik drops his head. "This isn't good," he mutters.

I can't help myself. "Why not?" I instantly regret asking. I feel as if I'm suffocating--I don't know how to handle this.

"Because marriage to a luna makes his pack stronger. It hurts our mission. There are lycans tasked with taking down packs, and this one is ours."

Reality sinks in at that moment, but I have to hold it together. People pepper the man with follow-up questions, but I can't stay, can't hear the answers to a single one. I think it might kill me. I excuse myself, going for the latrine. It's gross, nothing like the flushing toilets of Drayton Hall, but I'm no stranger to rough conditions. And it's the only place I can have some privacy.

Female guards stand far enough away to let me do my business, but I don't go to the hole in the ground that is our bathroom out here. Instead, I push past the latrine area, press up against the biggest tree I can find, and burst into tears.

Ryne is married.

CHAPTER 6

I lose track of time, the days dragging by. Even when we move our camp farther away from the wolf city in preparation for the upcoming new moon, I couldn't care less. Laik says not staying in one spot for long is for our protection. That, and the lycan can't fight very well during the new moon. He also says I have to help carry supplies since my wounds have healed.

Great. Don't care.

I'm grieving my old life, but most of all, I'm angry. The rage is all-consuming sometimes, and after we set up camp in our new location, I beg Laik to let me join the warriors. "Please," I plead, "I need to beat someone up." No one knows my connection to Ryne, but they have learned that I'm snappy and mean. I didn't used to be, but that's who I am now.

He turns to Knox, who is standing nearby. "Is she always like this?"

It's the first time he's addressed us together and it feels

like a trick. "Only since the wolf shifters murdered her twin sister in front of her and then took her in the claiming instead."

My cheeks flame, and I glare at Knox. I don't like my secrets aired out for people I don't trust, but Laik takes it all in stride. "Good." He nods to me. "Beat someone in a scrimmage, and I'll take you to the panther city with us tomorrow."

The panther city? Those three words wake me up. I didn't know there were other kinds of shifters until the conversation between Ryne and his father about overtaking the panther city. It's a conversation that feels like it happened a million years ago. That night we'd almost kissed, and then he'd kissed Faye instead to throw King Thorn off, but it had hurt all the same. I should've known then that a romance with Ryne was doomed. Of course, rumors of other shifters had abounded in my village growing up, but nobody could confirm anything. Now I know the truth, and whatever's in the panther city, I want to see it for myself.

"Deal."

"Better yet." He grins wickedly. "Knox, why don't you two fight? I don't even care who wins. I'll let you both come."

Knox scowls and backs away. "She's almost a lycan, and I'm not, which basically guarantees that she'll win. But even if she weren't, I wouldn't lay a finger on her." And then he walks away, which only makes Laik laugh. My anger isn't directed at Knox, but I'd definitely fight him if it meant we could both go tomorrow. Besides, the more the lycans see me and Knox around each other, the sooner we'll be allowed to talk again. And maybe get away from this horrible place.

I hate the camp. At first I'd thought maybe I could like it, or at least tolerate it, but the more time I spend here, the more time I want to get away. The days are monotonous--just a bunch of angry people waiting for the full moon so they can go do something. They hate the wolves, and I'm sure they're planning another attack, but they won't tell me anything. I haven't proven my loyalty to Laik, and I doubt I ever will.

I watch Knox disappear into the trees and want to scream at him to get back here, that I'm not a lycan yet, that I need him, but I don't get the chance. Someone jumps me from behind. Wanda laughs in my ear, her breath hot as she yanks on my braid. Fingers claw down my face as I throw her off me and round to face her.

"Let's see what you got, princess," she hisses. This woman is hot and cold, but the more Laik has loosened up on me, the colder she's gotten. I can't figure her out, and maybe that's the point. She doesn't want me to be able to guess what she's going to do next.

"How about a fair fight?" I snap.

She laughs at that. "You think the wolves will be fair?"

It's strange, this conversation. I had practically the same one with Ryne when I was first taken down to the basement of the manor and taught to fight. They'd jumped me then too.

"True," I say, punching her directly in the nose.

Wanda's voice drops into a low growl, and she lunges for me. I jump out of the way, and she goes stumbling in the crowd, which has now gathered around us like moths to a flame. Laik oversees us. His thick arms are crossed, and a nasty smirk mars his face.

"Beat Poppy, and you can go with us to the panther city tomorrow." He raises an eyebrow at his woman.

Their relationship is odd, and in the few seconds I've been paying attention to Laik, Wanda has regrouped. Before I can react, she tackles me to the ground.

Her putrid breath is worse than her fists pommeling my side. We have soap here and herbs to clean our teeth, but she must not care or she's done this on purpose to throw me off. I've never done well on my back, and her stench is disarming. I roll, knowing I'll take more hits, but it will also be easier for me to get up. She tumbles off me, and I jump to my feet. I don't know her strengths and weaknesses, and I don't want this fight to last long.

I don't even wait for her to get her bearings. I swing my leg up and around and manage to connect right with the side of her head. She crumples to the ground, unconscious.

My eyes flash to Laik's, and for a second I'm afraid he's going to be angry with me for taking down his mate, but instead a slow grin forms on his face.

"I told you I could fight," I say.

"Geoff and Malik, take Wanda to see Callum. Poppy, you've earned yourself a visit to the panther city. We leave at dawn."

* * *

I don't like leaving Knox behind, but I'm excited about our trip. I'm not excited about the walk, however.

"How far away is it?" I ask.

Laik adjusts his backpack. So far, it's just me and him. I was a little eager to make this journey but also a little nervous to be alone with this brute of a leader.

"About thirty miles."

I swallow down my groan. That will take all day. My feet are better, but I can already imagine the blisters I'll be dealing with soon.

Wanda approaches, glaring at me, but doesn't say anything. She has a purple bruise on the side of her face and a split lip. It makes her look even wilder than before. She runs her finger along the wounds and grins at me like she likes them. I didn't think about what it would mean to have her with us, but she might use this time to retaliate. I doubt she'd do anything in front of Laik, but she could easily make something look like an accident. What if she wants me dead?

"Who are we waiting for?" I ask Laik, turning away from Wanda.

"Just Callum. He needs to get some more medicine."

I haven't had a chance to hang out with Callum since that first day. Laik has kept me on gathering wood duty, which is nice because I get to wander in the woods. There's always another man with me, but they have all been quiet. I know it's because they don't trust me, and I normally wouldn't mind, but it has left me far too much time to think.

And the only one I ever think of is Ryne.

His betrayal eats away at my soul. I recognize that to him, I'm as good as dead, but it still hurts. I feel like I didn't know him or Elle at all. How they could do this to me--

still get married despite everything--is beyond my comprehension.

Callum joins us, rubbing his eyes, and I nudge him. "Not a morning person?"

As if on cue, he yawns. "Definitely not."

Laik starts walking with Wanda right behind him. I frown, so I guess she is coming along after all. I'll have to watch my back. Callum and I follow them, and for the first twenty minutes or so, we all walk in silence. Then the path opens up a bit, and Wanda falls in next to Laik, and Callum and I walk side by side.

"Do you like it here so far?" he asks.

Absolutely not. And with the full moon fast approaching, I hate it even more. The moon haunts my dreams, keeping me awake at night. "I don't know," I say instead. "I mean, at least I'm not worried I'll be sent to the mating house." I sigh heavily.

"But?" This time he nudges me, and something inside me unlocks.

"But it's not exactly comfortable living in the wilds knowing I'm going to turn into a monster soon," I blurt out.

Callum furrows his brow. "The wolves are the monsters, not us. I've treated several women we've rescued from the mating houses. I'm glad you never went to one."

I think about that for a minute, twisting the information around in my head like a key I didn't know existed. "Rescue?" I always thought they turned them or killed them.

Callum nods as if the answer is obvious. "We work

closely with the Resistance to rescue as many women as possible."

This is the first I'm hearing about that, but I guess it makes sense considering everything I've seen. The lycans would kill the wolves, but they'd take the girls. Well, except for Charlotte. Not for the first time, I wonder if she's still alive.

"No offense, but what I've witnessed of those rescues haven't exactly gone to plan. My roommate got bit by a lycan and killed two other girls the next month during her renewal. I've also never heard of the lycan working with the Resistance, and my friend was one of them."

Callum's frown is thoughtful. "Nothing's perfect, so sometimes humans get bit, but we figure it's better they become lycan than be trapped as wolf baby-makers."

I'm not certain I agree with him, but I don't argue.

"How much do you know about the Resistance?" I ask. Maybe I can finally get the answers I've been seeking.

"Not much. I'm not in leadership. Laik is usually the only one who meets with them."

Laik turns abruptly, tromping off the path and into the dense woods. Callum and I scramble after him. We come to a small clearing where Laik is lifting a camouflaged tarp off a vehicle. There are several others here too. All hidden so well I wouldn't have realized they were here unless I was standing right in front of them.

"You have cars?" I ask, relief flooding my body.

Laik gives me a grin. "You didn't think we were walking the whole way, did you?"

Suddenly, my day just got a hundred times better.

Funny how I'd never even seen a car until I got to the

city, but now I've come to expect them on long journeys. This car is different from most of the ones in the wolf city. It's large, with two seats up front and an open compartment in the back. It kinda reminds me of a small boat.

"We'll climb in the bed," Callum offers. He reaches out a hand and helps me into the back, which is apparently the bed. It's the opposite of a bed, if you ask me. Sure, it's flat, but it's metal and uncomfortable. I'm still taking it all in when he chuckles. "You've never seen a truck, have you?"

"Nope. I didn't know that's what these cars are called." I swallow hard, the memories coming at me. "The first day in the wolf city, they put us on what they called a trailer bed. It was behind one of these. Then they drove us around the city to show us off to all the men."

A shadow passes over his face, making him look years older. "See? What did I say? They're the monsters, not us."

I'm beginning to wonder if he's right. Thorn is certainly a monster. But Ryne isn't. I clench my fists. Maybe he is. After all, he did go and marry Elle even though I'm his fated. Maybe everything I know about Ryne is a lie.

We sit down, Laik starts the engine, and we pull away, following the bumpiest dirt road I've ever seen. I'm tossed about and hanging onto the side for dear life. This is still way better than walking even though the engine is loud and the metal of the truck bed hurts my butt. The discomfort is nothing compared to the worry that creeps into my thoughts about where we're going.

What am I going to find in panther city?

CHAPTER 7

We have to pass through a wasteland to get to the panther city. I knew it was bad out here in the wilds, but to see it for myself is chilling. There are no more trees. For miles, there's nothing out here but barren wilderness.The humans had nuked various areas to try to take out the shifters. Turned out humans were the only ones who were affected by the bombs, but it left scars all over the landscapes. I've never crossed a radioactive field before.

"This is the most dangerous part," Callum says over the rumble of tires. "We've had a lot of scrimmages with the wolves out here because we're so open to attack."

"If they're hunting you, why stay near them at all?" It seems to me that the lycans could find everything they need in the woods. Or find a home far away from the wolf shifters, like with the panthers or some other friendly pack.

He gives me a hard stare. "It's our choice to be in the

camps. We could stay with the panthers and live normal lives, but all of us have reasons to put ourselves in danger."

Two things stick out to me. One, that he said camps, meaning more than one. Could Joanna and Grady be in a different camp of lycans? But no, that doesn't make sense. Grady is a wolf shifter--they'd never take him in. And two, that Callum has a reason to be out here risking his life. I imagine what they're doing is like being on the front lines of a war. And he's so young. So many of us never had any choices, but it seems he did. He could die before ever really getting a chance to live.

We hit a big pothole, and I scream a little, then immediately feel stupid. "Is the area still radioactive?" I ask, wanting to deflect my embarrassment and because it would be good to know.

"Sure is," he says, "but you don't need to worry about that. The only ones who are affected by that are the humans, and you'll be a lycan in a few weeks anyway. When we have humans with us, we have to go around the radiation hotspots. It takes way longer, but we don't want to risk them getting sick."

My heart sinks because it's one more reminder of what I'm going to become. When I first arrived here, I hoped to find a cure to the venom. It's only taken a few weeks for me to completely give that notion up. It's happening whether I want it to or not. And now that Laik is purposely exposing me to radiation, what other choice do I have? Anger is my first emotion, but it's only on the surface. There's something much deeper hidden underneath, and that's grief.

Again, my mind returns to Joanna. Has she been

exposed to something like this? I hope she's okay. My heart aches, wanting to know where they are and what they're doing. Grady lost his arm and may have bled out. For all I know, he's dead, and she could be too.

I don't ask Callum any more questions after that. The dead zone fades into the distance, and the forest returns. It's denser now, the vegetation thicker than it is on the other side of the zone. There's always humidity in the air, but I feel it growing as if we're getting closer to the ocean. Even though our rivers feed into it, I've never actually seen the ocean before. Maybe I finally will. Something about that makes me incredibly sad, missing all the people I've lost. I could be experiencing something new that they'll never get to experience with me. My little brother Evan would've loved it. Actually, my whole family would've had the time of their lives. I can picture Willow running head-first into the water like she always did, little Evan close behind her, and my parents standing watch with satisfied grins on their faces. And I'd be there too, content and happy and soaking it all in. I can see it all--a nice fantasy that will never exist.

We pull up to a guard station, and someone stops us to talk to Laik. The man has a big gun strapped across his bare chest and black shorts on. It's only April, but it's warming up, and I've learned that shifters aren't as sensitive to extreme temperatures as humans. The man waves us through, and as we pass, his dark eyes meet mine.

He pities me, and I wonder why. Is his life really so much better? We're all scrambling to survive in the same harsh world.

We drive into a city that feels much like the wolf city.

Some of the buildings are abandoned and lost to the wars, but the ones that aren't are well taken care of. People come out of their homes to watch us, some of them even waving and calling out warm greetings. Is this the place that Ryne talked about with his dad? The one he wanted to take over for his pack? I shiver at the thought of these people being forced into the wolves' cruel system. As much as I'll always love Ryne, I'm not a fool. I know what they are doing there is wrong. Someone has to make it stop. Maybe the lycan aren't as bad as I thought they were. It's hard to imagine being one of them, but it's happening soon. I would stay and help, but I don't know if I can stomach fighting against Ryne. Just seeing him again would break me.

Thinking of Ryne reminds me of the wedding, and my heart stills. I can't love Ryne anymore. I have to make myself stop. It would be so much easier to hate him, but I can't seem to do that either. I'm doomed to a broken heart.

We pull to a stop next to a park, and Laik jumps out, coming around to pat the side of the truck. "Welcome to Savannah," he says, his tone lighter than I've ever heard. "The northernmost city in the panther shifter territory. Are you ready to prove your loyalty yet?"

My mouth falls open, and he laughs. "Just kidding. I'll save that for after your first renewal."

I glare, thinking of a few choice words, but I keep them to myself. If he dumps me here in this city, then I'll never see my family or friends again. Am I ready for that? It's a reality I haven't accepted yet even though I know it's one I'm currently living.

No. It's best to follow along and make him think I respect him, even though he's done nothing to earn my trust. Even if these guys have a worthy mission, I don't like the way he lords over everyone or the way he keeps me and Knox from talking. His power trip is growing exhausting, and his mate has a few screws loose. Even now, Wanda is watching me like she's planning my death. Her smile is sinister, and her eyes sparkle with mischief. "Come," he says, taking off for a nearby building. Like the little mindless followers that he thinks we are, we hurry after him.

Callum grabs my hand. "I'm going to take Poppy to get medical supplies."

Laik pulls out a few coins, giving them to Callum. "Meet back here in two hours. Get some lunch as well."

Callum nods and drags me away from Laik and Wanda. It's an immediate relief, especially when Wanda's face falls. Whatever she was planning will have to wait.

I'm a bit in awe as we walk down the street. The people here are so . . . content. No one is fearing for their lives, and men and women mingle freely. Kids run up and down the streets as well. They're not dressed as nicely as the betas and their wives, nor as poorly as the lower-ranked wolves. They remind me a lot of the people in my village, simple and hardworking. But there's a sense of happiness that I haven't seen anywhere before. I almost don't trust it.

"After we finish getting the supplies I need, we'll get some food." Callum tightens his hand around mine. "Savannah has the best shrimp and grits in the world."

"What's shrimp?" I ask.

He laughs, mirth dancing in his eyes. "You'll see."

We stop outside a shop that has a line out the door, and Callum joins it.

"What's this?" I ask, eyeing the brick building with

Pharmacy written across the top. I don't know what it means, except that it must be something medical if Callum is here.

"We're getting more antibiotics. Savannah has one of the only labs in the area that can make them. They have a limited supply, so they only sell so much per person each day. Even the doctors in the city have to come for refills often. I wish we could travel here more often to get them, but Laik and the panthers have a deal that we can only come once a month."

"Why only once a month?"

"It's dangerous." We move up the line, and he nods toward the building. "But necessary. Even though lycans can usually fight off infections naturally, sometimes antibiotics are needed to save a life."

It's that word again, "antibiotics." Maybe I should ask him what it does, but from what I can piece together, it must be something to heal these infections he speaks of. I don't know what he means by the word "lab" either. I people-watch while we stand in line, and those questions get filtered out by more interesting ones. There is a vendor with all kinds of delicious fruits across the street. I recognize most of them--apples, oranges, and bananas. But there are others that I've never seen before. My mouth waters just looking at them.

A young couple, with a boy who looks to be about three, approaches the fruit stand and chats with the vendor. The man has his arm slung loosely over the woman's shoulder, and she laughs at something the vendor says.

It's only then that I recognize the different types of

people. Some are as tall as the wolves, but most are not. People are dressed in a multitude of styles, and skin color ranges from light pale to dark brown to black. I've never seen such diversity.

I go back to watching the young couple. The little boy grabs a strawberry and shoves it in his mouth while no one is looking. His mother glances down and sees the red juice streaming down his chin.

She scolds him, and without warning, his clothes go flying, and he turns into a tiny panther. He has an adorable black face and black spots, but he growls and snaps at his mother. His father immediately shifts into a much larger panther, his coat a glossy black, and lays a heavy paw on top of the boy's head, snarling and growling.

Then, just as quickly as it began, they both shift back. The mother grumbles, handing them fresh clothing from her satchel, and they quickly dress. The little boy wipes a few tears from his face as his mother gathers him in her arms, and he buries his face in her hair. It's an embrace I've seen countless times before. Human or not, we all need our parents to love us.

Except the wolves--most of them don't have parents. They only have the pack. Maybe that's why they're so ruthless? They're raised without love.

The little family turns back and continues their conversation with the vendor as if nothing has happened.

Callum nudges me. "Panthers are taught to respect women from a very young age. It's different from the wolves, yeah?"

"It is. Is the whole city made up of panther shifters and their families?"

"It used to be, but it's become a sanctuary of sorts. The majority of the population is panther, but they welcome almost anyone, so besides humans, you'll find lycans and a few of the exiled wolves who plead their case successfully. I've even heard there are even some shifters from out west, like bears and hawks, but I've never met one."

I wonder if maybe Joanna and Grady made it here. I wish there was a way for me to search for them, but I wouldn't even know where to start.

The line moves slowly, but eventually we get inside the shop.

Two men in white coats stand behind a counter.

Callum approaches. "I'm from Laik's camp."

One of the men nods and flips through a book. He runs a finger down the page. "It says here you have about twenty people, and you are thirty miles away. Is that correct?"

"Yes, sir."

"And did you use all of your medicine?"

"No. I still have two bottles left. But last month we ran out."

"Very well. Give him four bottles."

The other man gives Callum a bag, and we head back out on the bustling street.

"You didn't give him any coins," I say.

"We don't pay for medicine. The coins Laik gave me were for food. Speaking of . . ."

Callum stops at a vendor that has small caramel-colored candies. He picks up a couple and hands me one. "These are amazing."

I taste one, and sweetness explodes in my mouth. I've had decent desserts at Drayton Hall, but candy isn't something I've eaten a lot of before. The sugar melts in my mouth and the nuts at the center stick to my teeth. Once I've managed to eat it all, I laugh. "What is that stuff?"

"Pralines." He glances at a clock on the wall. "We gotta hurry if we're going to get all that we need. You know the food we eat back at camp isn't the best, so the days we come to Savannah, we get something more tasty to bring back for dinner. It keeps the others from getting too jealous that they weren't invited to come along."

We dodge in and out of the crowd, which seems to grow thicker as we get farther into the city. I also see several panthers lounging about in the streets or sidewalks. It's just so different from the wolf city.

Everyone here is relaxed. I don't see any indication of extreme wealth or extreme poverty--just all kinds of people working and living together. I can't believe that Ryne would consider taking over this place. That would be barbaric. Maybe I've completely misjudged him.

Maybe he is the enemy.

CHAPTER 8

"Why wouldn't you want to stay here?" I question Callum after we've gathered the last of our supplies and stopped to scarf down the yummy shrimp and grits. "This is so much better than living in the wilds." I motion to the lively city square. There's electricity and running water and happy people. "I don't get it."

"Someone has to protect all this."

"But why can't the panthers do that?"

He swallows hard and looks around, as if making sure nobody is eavesdropping. I don't think anyone is. We're two of many here, and nobody seems to pay us any mind. "They have a cease-fire treaty with the wolves and aren't willing to fight them unless absolutely necessary. It's why Laik says we can only come here once a month. Because he wants to keep our business with the panthers a secret."

"So you're doing their dirty work for them." It's actually pretty smart, but for some reason it irks me, and it shouldn't. I want to end the human slavery as much as these people do, but I can't help but think of Ryne getting killed by the end of all this. My alliances are muddled, and it's starting to wear on me. I need to let him go already.

Because the lycans are right.

"The panthers are run similar to the wolves with several cities working together. They have guards who protect those cities," Callum continues, "but they don't send soldiers out to fight. They want to keep the peace they have here, and part of that means not starting any wars."

"Well, maybe they should," I grumble. I realize I've come to side with the lycans over the wolves. Hopefully that doesn't change after my first renewal, but I don't think it will. Even if I don't stay with Laik's people, I'll never be able to forget everything I've been through. If it wasn't for the wolves' brutality, I'd still have my family. I'd have a normal life.

"We have a few more minutes." Callum tucks my arm in his and leads me away. "There's something I want to show you, but you have to promise not to tell Laik."

We head toward one of the unmarked buildings, and my apprehension builds at keeping a secret from Laik. He still scares me, and Wanda is his match in every way. There's something strange about those two, like they belong out in the wilds instead of in the safety of the city.

"Laik wants you to stay with our camp," Callum says, "and he doesn't want you to know that you actually have a choice in the matter."

Before I can utter a response, Callum sweeps me through a doorway and into a beautiful lobby with polished marble floors and gleaming gilded mirrors. A man and a woman stand behind a desk, smiling warmly at us. "Welcome to The Sanctuary," the woman says. "How can we help you?"

"I'm here to give my friend a tour to see if she wants to stay here instead of with us in the wilds."

Her eyes widen, and she rushes toward me. "Oh, you poor thing! When did you get out?" She pats my cheeks and peers down at my weather-worn clothing. "Have you been with the lycans for long?"

"She's one of the claimed girls and was bitten during the last moon," Callum says. "She's been with us for a little over three weeks."

The woman steps back and nods solemnly. "In that case, we'd better start on the fourth floor."

"What's on the fourth floor?" My voice trembles. I don't like the pitying way everyone is looking at me. I know my life isn't perfect, and I've been victimized, but I don't need pity from anyone. It makes me feel weaker than I already am.

"People who understand exactly what you're going through," she says, and I stiffen. How could anyone truly understand the ache of my heart? I've been alone since the moment I lost my twin, and I don't expect that to ever change. "I'm sorry, but you'll have to wait here. There are no men allowed past the lobby," she explains to Callum.

"No problem, just have her back in ten minutes if you can. We're short on time."

"In that case . . ." She turns around, her long skirt swishing at her ankles, and hurries toward the staircase while I follow. My thighs are burning by the time we get all the way up to the fourth floor, but that pain is nothing compared to my curiosity.

"The Sanctuary is for the women who come from the wolf cities. Most of them have been in the mating houses and have a lot of trauma to work through before they're comfortable around men again, which is why I asked your friend to stay behind."

Okay, so maybe they do understand bits of my heartache. My virtue was never ripped from me, but my sister and my friends were. And my love betrayed me in the most painful way. They're all wounds that can never be fully healed, but maybe these people can make it so they don't fester so badly.

The woman throws open a set of double doors, and light streams over my face, then my eyes adjust, and I take it all in. The large sitting room, the kitchen tucked to the side, the lines of doors leading to what I assume are bedrooms, and the women.

Young women.

"This floor is reserved specifically for women like you--women who've escaped the wolves but not the lycan. Everyone here has already been through a renewal. You could choose to stay if you wanted. I can tell your friend that you're not leaving with him."

I blink, letting her words sink in. It would be so easy . . .

One by one, the ladies turn toward us, some smiling and waving, others offering consolatory nods. And then one in particular turns from where she's standing at the window, her honey-blonde hair lit up like a halo.

I freeze--a torrent of emotions storming through me, anger and sadness and frustration all at once. I would recognize that girl anywhere. "Charlotte," I say at the same time she whispers my name. Something comes over me, as if I'm not myself. I march toward her and slap her clean across her face. Hard.

Time stops, and nobody moves.

And then all at once, I'm descended upon by people trying to stop me, but I don't care. All I care about is Charlotte and the horrible things she did. "How could you?" I start screaming, fighting against the strength of a powerful lycan woman holding me back. "You killed so many of us! You kept your bite a secret from me."

"Let her go," Charlotte orders the women, her voice stoic. A tear drops from her eye, and my desire to punish her weakens. "She's right. I deserved that."

"No." Someone tightens her hold on me. "You never asked to be bit."

"If you'd told anyone, you'd have died," another adds.

Charlotte glares at them, and they loosen their grip. I shake free. "Are you saying that her life is more valuable than the others who died because of her actions?" I glare at the women. If this is the attitude they have, then maybe I don't want to stay at this sanctuary. "Let's see, you ripped those girls to shreds, you killed one of our house mothers, and you bit another who had to be put down by Anders. Is there anyone else I'm forgetting? Any others you've taken out since that night?"

"You're right," Charlotte says again, stepping toward me. More tears roll down her face. This isn't the Charlotte I knew. Where's the selfishness? Where's the cold shoulder and the prissy attitude? I suddenly feel bad for the things I've said, but I shouldn't because I'm right. Why should she be forgiven so easily when she could've told someone she'd been bitten? She chose herself over all of us, and it cost several people their lives.

"I made a mistake, and it's something I will have to live the rest of my life regretting. But you're here now, so I'm guessing you've been bitten too."

I meet her eyes and harden my voice. "Yes. But I haven't killed anyone." I practically spit out the words. "And I'd rather die than do what you did."

"Then let me help you," she rushes out. "I'll make sure what happened to me doesn't happen to you also."

I step back. I want nothing to do with this woman. I've had a lot of time to think about this, and I know in my heart of hearts that I couldn't do what she did. Fortunately though, when I shift for the first time, I'll be surrounded by lycan. I don't need Charlotte. "I'm sorry, but it's too late for you to absolve yourself. Those women are already dead, and I already have people who are going to help me."

I turn back to the woman who brought me up here. Her mouth is set in an angry line. Maybe she thinks I'm being too harsh on Charlotte, and maybe I am, but I don't care. She had so many opportunities to tell the truth. And if she'd told me, I would've helped her get out of Drayton Hall somehow. It's not like I would've just turned her into the wolves. But she went into that locked room knowing full-well she was going to turn into a lycan, and in doing so, she knowingly chose her own life over so many others. If that's what they condone here at The Sanctuary, if they're okay with her living a great life without any punishment for what she did to us, then I don't want it.

"I'm ready to go back to my friend now," I say, heading

for the staircase. The woman follows behind, and there's another set of footsteps behind that.

"I'm going with you," Charlotte says.

I whip back around and glare up at her.

"It's a lycan camp out in the wilds," the woman interrupts. "It's no place for a young lady, Charlotte."

"Wherever you're going and whatever you're doing," she continues, ignoring the woman and pinning her crystal-blue eyes on me. "I have to try to make up for what I did."

"I don't want you there," I spit out and bunch my hands into fists. I'll fight her if I have to.

Her eyes water again, and she clears her throat. "Too bad."

"No."

"Please," she whispers, "please, let me at least try to pay penance for what I did." Her voice cracks, and the pain is unmistakable. "I know it was wrong, okay? I know that. But I was scared and dumb, and I made a mistake. Haven't you ever made a mistake?"

Not one that got people killed.

Her pleas seep through me, but my resolve is firm. "If you come back with me, it's not because I'm okay with it or because I forgive you."

"I don't expect--"

"And my friend brought me to The Sanctuary when he wasn't supposed to. You're going to get us in trouble. Stay here, Charlotte. You're not wanted anywhere else."

Those are cruel words, and I expect her to deflate with them, but she doesn't. She stands even taller, her mind made up. "I'll tell your people that I ran into you in the city. Nobody has to know you stopped by The Sanctuary."

I roll my eyes. This girl really has an excuse for everything, doesn't she? I let her walk all over me, but I won't do it anymore. I'm done with Charlotte. However, it appears that she isn't done with me.

"You follow me, and you're going to have to convince Laik that you're worth his time. Good luck with that one."

"Who's Laik?" She folds her arms over her chest as if she's up for the challenge. But I meant what I said--I'm done. I turn to leave, fully prepared for her to follow me against my wishes. The woman has made up her mind. I can't stop her when she's like this, but I don't have to give her any warnings about Laik either, let alone Wanda. She's about to find out what it's like to be on the receiving end of a very distrustful bunch of lycans.

CHAPTER 9

"No, absolutely not." Laik crosses his arms over his chest. We're standing next to the truck, and I don't even bother to deal with whatever is going to come of this. I climb into the bed and wait for this conversation to be settled.

"Why not?" Charlotte asks, brows furrowing. She's got that innocent look about her that I know is complete crap, but always seems to work in her favor. "I can fight. And you people come in all the time asking for more fighters. You need me. Why would you say no?"

"Other camps might come looking for more fighters, but I don't. Our camp is different. I trust everyone, and I don't trust you."

Well, that's interesting, considering Laik has made it abundantly clear that he doesn't trust me. So why is he keeping me around? There's still something I'm missing . . .

Charlotte throws her hands in the air. "You trust

Poppy? I thought she just joined your little group. If she could prove herself, then so can I."

"Hey," I call out, "leave me out of it."

"Actually, I don't trust Poppy yet." He turns to give me a scowl, and I roll my eyes. "But she'll get the opportunity to prove herself after her first renewal. She brings certain . . . qualities to our camp that I'm looking for."

My qualities? What qualities? Something about that word and the way he said it leaves me uneasy.

"Let her come," Wanda interrupts dryly.

Laik spins on her. "Why?"

"We have too many men and not enough women. It's causing fights. Another woman should ease the tensions for a bit." Her reasoning makes sense, even if it does make my skin crawl a little.

"That's not why I want to go." Charlotte's blue eyes widen, but nobody seems to care.

"Look, Poppy's already gained the attention of Callum, and now he and Delson aren't fighting over Rachel," Wanda goes on. "We need more women, you've said so yourself."

Callum's ears go pink, but I don't care about that right now. "You aren't bringing Charlotte into your camp just to use her like the wolves do at the mating houses," I growl, jumping out of the truck bed and pointing at them. "That's not why I'm there, is it?"

Laik storms up to me, getting right into my face. "We may live like wild animals in the woods, but we treat our women with respect. Not a single one is forced or coerced to do anything, and don't you dare accuse us of such brutality." He takes a step away and turns to Charlotte.

"Why do you really want to join us? And don't lie to me." He looks her up and down, "A woman like you doesn't seem like the type, lycan or not."

She stands taller, and her blonde curls bounce around her shoulders. He's right. Charlotte is nothing like the people in our camp. She's way too prissy, and I know she'll be begging to leave within a week. "Because it's an opportunity to get back at the wolves," she says with conviction. "I've been hiding out here since I escaped, but I want nothing more than to bring those dogs down."

Laik studies her for a long moment, then gives a stiff nod. "Fine, you can join us. But remember that I'll be watching you. Give me one reason to doubt your loyalty, and you're gone."

Callum, Charlotte, and I climb back into the bed of the truck, which is now full of all kinds of supplies. Callum sits on the opposite side of the truck from Charlotte and I but doesn't look me in the eye. Maybe he wanted me to stay at The Sanctuary? Maybe he's upset that I have another confidant now? Or is he embarrassed that Wanda said he was interested in me? I'm not sure, but I don't have the time or the energy to figure it out.

"Are you okay?" Charlotte whispers to me once the truck starts up.

"Why wouldn't I be?" I snap, and she raises a knowing eyebrow.

"You've been bit. Also, you were at the bottom of the leaderboards before I left. Were you in the mating house?" Her voice softens. "I've heard horrible stories from those places."

I shake my head. "Not that it's any of your business, but

I managed to keep myself at Drayton Hall. I was supposed to marry Nico the night I was bit." My insides go sour because that's not the whole truth. I wish I could tell her everything, but I can't, and I never will. She's not trustworthy. And if I can't talk about it, it's almost as if it never happened.

"Nico. Huh. He seemed like a nice guy. But you know they're all monsters, right? The wolf packs need to be taken out. If we can do that, we might be able to live in peace."

I wince at the thought of taking them all out. Is killing them all the answer? It seems too extreme. What about the children? Or the ones who don't hurt anybody? If we condemn them all because of what they are, then we'll become the bigger monsters.

"What about the lycans?" I ask. "It's not like they're innocent--you should know."

She shrugs, and her pretty blue eyes go cloudy. "You learn to control it. Each renewal is easier than the last. And as long as you're not a bastard like I was, you never have to bite or kill anyone except for the wolves. The first couple of shifts are really hard, but you'll have support to help you through it, and after that, it's easy."

"Then how did you get bit?" I scoff. That first night in the city was terrifying, no thanks to them. "If they have such control, why bite a human girl?"

"Because sometimes the lycan make mistakes," Callum interrupts. I didn't realize he was listening to our conversation. "We're not perfect, but we're doing the best we can."

Charlotte nods.

"I don't understand how you can defend against biting like that."

Something clicks in his jaw, like I've pushed a sensitive button. "Look, we go into the cities on the full moon to kill as many wolf shifters as we can and to rescue humans. But when you're in the midst of fighting, sometimes there are casualties. Innocent people get bit. It doesn't happen very often, but it does happen. We usually take them straight to panther city to get help."

My mind races back to that night and the two girls who were taken. "Is that what happened to those other claimed girls back on the harvest night? Were they rescued?"

"Yes." He nods, like that's a sufficient answer. "And they weren't even bit. I'm pretty sure Charlotte here was the only mistake that night."

I try to remember it, to see if he's telling the truth, but my memories of that horrible night are all muddled. Too much has happened.

"Then why didn't Laik take me to The Sanctuary?" I ask. "Why go to all the trouble of keeping me in the camp and separating me from Knox? Why enroll us into your cause without even asking us first?"

Callum considers this for a long second before finally shaking his head. "I don't know. He should've taken you to The Sanctuary right away, and Knox could've found a new life too. But whatever you said to him during your interrogation changed his mind. He obviously thinks you can help us in some way."

My heart sinks. Does he know then? Is this all because of Ryne? If Laik knows I'm Ryne's fated mate, it could change everything. All this time I've been thinking nobody knows who I really am, but what if they've been playing me? I think back to when Laik had me trapped in that tent, but I was so scared that I don't remember what I said.

"About what Wanda said about Delson and me," Callum mutters, and I wave a hand.

"It doesn't matter."

"No. It does. I don't want you to think that my friendship is manipulative."

Charlotte's lips curl into a small smile as she looks away. It's not like it's real privacy though, and I don't want to have this conversation anyway.

"I know it's not manipulative, and it's okay. We're friends." I wonder for a second what it would be like to be in a romantic relationship with someone like Callum. He's kind and cute, not brutish in any way. He's a little younger than me, but lots of girls back at the village dated younger boys. And Callum reminds me of Knox in a lot of ways, which is a good thing. But my heart still belongs to Ryne, as much as I don't want it to. And if I were to give it to anyone else, I can't help but think that person *would* be Knox. I know I'll never have Ryne, and Knox would probably take me back, but how do I turn off my feelings for someone that was chosen for me by fate? Maybe I should pursue someone else. Maybe a different man could help me remember what it's like to love for real. Even though my heart wants Ryne and my past lies with Knox, maybe Callum is the safest choice for my future. He doesn't know about my history or my secrets, doesn't have expectations of me, and is eager to please.

I don't know if my heart can move on, but I decide I'd better try because otherwise I'm afraid Ryne's betrayal is going to fester and eat me alive. I worry a little bit about what Knox might think, but since I can't talk to him right now, this is the best I'm going to do.

I leave Charlotte's side and make it over to Callum without falling over. I sit close to him, like I would if this were one of my dates with the betas. He gives me a shy smile, and I wait for that familiar swoop of desire, but it never comes.

CHAPTER 10

The days leading up to the full moon are fraught with worry. I can feel the lycanthrope virus growing stronger with the phases of the moon and can't deny that I'll soon belong to it. As much as I wanted to believe I'd somehow be different--that there was no possible way I'd turn--that was wishful thinking.

I sit up on the cot, skin wet with chilly sweat, and gasp for air. The women around me stir, but none wake. They all know about my nightmares by now. The dreams always feature sharp teeth, long claws, and grotesque limbs. Sometimes Ryne is there. Or my parents. Sometimes Willow or my brother. Once, I dreamed about the claimed girls, about Joanna and Faye and the ones who'd been taken to the mating houses already. But the dreams always end the same, with me turning into a monster and hurting people.

I crawl from the tent, and my heart rate slows as the night air calms me. I wander over to the hole-in-the-ground bathroom to relieve myself and then walk back to the tent. I stare at it for several long minutes. I can't bring myself to go back to bed just yet. I can't go outside of the perimeter of the camp without getting stopped by one of Laik's guards, so I sit by the campfire instead. There's nothing left but a few glowing coals. I sink down onto a stump and let my mind go. It's been so hot lately, but right now it's not. I shiver in the chilly night air and think about starting the fire up again, but I don't have the energy.

We pack up our camp and move through the forest every five or six days. Laik says it's to stay safe from the wolves, which is probably true, but I also think it's to keep the members of the camp from fighting. We have to stay busy. Since arriving, Charlotte has become a favorite, fitting in much easier than I ever did. She's tried to reach out to me, but I want nothing to do with her. She can pay her penance to someone else. Not to mention, within hours of coming back with us from the panther city, she'd rekindled her friendship with Knox. I don't have ownership over him, but it bothers me to see them together. He should be on my side, not hers.

Footsteps approach, and Knox sits next to me. His hair is a mess of blonde haloing his head now that it's starting to grow back out, and his clothes are rumpled from sleep.

"We're not supposed to be seen together," I mutter.

"I don't care anymore." He drags his boot along the ground, forming a line in the dirt between us. "I think Laik is more bark than bite."

I snort. "Don't let him hear you say that."

He looks up, taking in the inky sky with the big round moon in the middle. "What are you going to do, Poppy?"

I look up too. The full moon is tomorrow night, but it's

so big right now that I can almost pretend it's tonight and that I'm still human, that I made it out unscathed, and the bite did nothing. "I don't think there's anything I can do." I have no idea what he expects of me. I have no choice about turning, and I hate that. I'm so tired of having my choices ripped away from me. It's like no matter what I do, there will always be something else directing my fate.

"I'm not talking about becoming a lycan. I'm talking about Ryne."

At that, I shush him and look around.

"Nobody's here but you and me." He points out. "Are you going to try and go back to him?"

"What do you mean? He sent me out here and betrayed me," I say darkly. "You saw what happened. As far as I'm concerned, things with Ryne are over, and I wouldn't go back to him even if I had the chance. If I never see his face again, I won't be sad." But even as I say the words, I know they are nothing but lies. I shove away my love for Ryne and focus on my hate instead. That's easier right now.

"He also saved you. Any other wolf would've killed you the second they saw that bite."

I press my lips together. "Why are you defending him? You should hate the wolves as much as anyone."

"And I do," he says, "but this conversation isn't about me. It's about you."

"I don't get where you're going with this." But maybe I do, and my skin starts to prickle all over with awareness.

"I know you love Ryne, but are you still going to be on his side, even after your renewal tomorrow?"

He knows a lot about my relationship with the alpha and knows I'm fated to Ryne, but I'm not sure he fully understands what that means. He saw way too much, but I'm suddenly glad he did. "You were there for a lot of it, and I'm sorry for that." I swallow hard. "But you still don't know what it's like to be fated to one of them. You don't know that kind of all-consuming love."

"I don't?" he snaps, and then he's on his knees before me, grabbing my hands between his, and my world flips upside down. "Because I'd take you back in a heartbeat. I've been hurting for so long, and you're the only one who can heal my heart."

Back in our village, we had talked about running away together before he had to go to the claiming. Ultimately we didn't because our families would've been punished for it. Although we did love each other, it was a shadow of what I had with Ryne.

"Knox, I don't know . . ."

His face twists in agony. "Please, just listen to me. I've had to watch you from a distance for the last month, knowing the kind of pain you were going through and not being able to talk to you. Not only that, but from the moment I saw you in the city, I had hope that we could be together once again.

"First I had you, then I lost you, then I thought I had you again, but I had to watch you fall in love with someone else. And even though I know you'll always love him, I still don't care. I still want you. You're the girl for me. There's never been anyone else, and there never will be."

My heart speeds at his words, but my stomach goes hollow. His confession could make things easy for me. I could give into this new life without looking back. And I so desperately want to give him what he wants, but I can't. In my heart of hearts, I know he deserves better.

I pull my hands away and stand. "I'm sorry, Knox, but I'm not your girl." I'm rejecting him for his sake, not my own. Ryne will never be mine, not now that he's married to Elle, but the history between Knox and me is just too heavy. He knows too much. And as much as I could give into this, I don't want to do that to my friend.

"So, what? You're just going to find an oblivious guy like Callum?" His voice is hollow as he stands. He's taller than me, but it's not like when Ryne towers over me. I don't feel a burning in my chest or a need to be near him. I don't love him anymore. That much I know. "Because he'll never love you the way I can. Nobody else here could possibly feel what I feel. I know you, Poppy. We're good together. I'll fix your broken heart, I swear." His voice has risen slightly, and I worry that he's going to wake someone, but I don't move away or shush him. I may never be able to love Knox romantically, but I do want to be his friend. He's the only one who could possibly understand my situation.

He reaches out and traces the line of my cheek. I don't realize I'm crying until his fingers are mopping up my hot tears. His skin is cool and perfect, and I almost give in. Maybe I could do it. Maybe I could let him try to fix me. But what happens tomorrow? Or a year from now? Ten years from now?

"I'm sorry," I whisper, "but I care about you too much to let you try. The truth is, eventually we'll both end up hurt because how can we be together when my heart is beyond repair? And even if you stayed with me, you would come to resent that I don't love you the same way. I don't want that for you, Knox. I want you to have the kind of love I thought I did. You will find it."

And with those words spoken aloud, I realize how foolish I was to think I could try to flirt with other guys and maybe date someone else. It's impossible that there could be anyone but Ryne. Maybe eventually this feeling will fade, but right now it's hot and all-consuming. Even after a month apart, it hasn't gone away. It's only grown stronger. The memory that he tried to kill my friends and then threw me out in the cold when I needed him most is the only thing that's going to get me through my renewal tomorrow night. I'm angry, and I'm starting to hate Ryne even more than I love him.

Knox's face falls in disappointment, but he doesn't look surprised either. He steps back, his head hanging low.

"And to answer your earlier question..." I clear my throat and fold my arms over my chest, resolve spreading through every inch of me. "I am *not* on the wolves' side. I never was, and I never will be."

"What's that supposed to mean? You just told me you could never love me because you still love him."

I grab his hand. "I do, but I also hate him. Can you understand that? Sometimes love and hate get tangled together."

"Yes." He swallows. My heart drops, and he squeezes my hand. "I don't hate you, Poppy. I never could. And I hate Ryne too, but I also worry about him. I know a little about what you're feeling. I was a slave, and I didn't have a choice in that, but he treated me fairly." He shrugs. "It's hard to explain, but my gut tells me Ryne isn't all bad. Still, he's the alpha, so he's responsible for what's happening there."

Is he? Or is Thorn? Either way, I don't want to talk about Ryne anymore, so I change the subject. "Are we going to listen to Laik or not?"

He drops my hand. "What do you mean?"

"Well, he said we weren't even allowed to look at each other, but here we are alone in the middle of the night. As I see it, we have three options: we could run away, we could go back to bed and pretend that we didn't have this conversation, or we can hang out here and tell Laik to jump in the lake."

Knox snorts. "My vote is number three. I'd say number one, but you are going to turn into one of them tomorrow night, and I'm not sure I want to be alone with you when that happens."

He has a point. Part of me had hoped he'd run away with me because I still don't really feel comfortable here, but it's too late for all that.

"Okay, so what do you say we start the fire up? Pretty sure I'm not getting any more sleep tonight."

Knox doesn't answer, but he starts gathering up the wood. I help him, all the while trying hopelessly not to think about what tomorrow will bring.

CHAPTER 11

I sit with Knox and Charlotte at breakfast, and it's almost like being at home again. Callum sits on the other side of me, and I don't remember ever having a more enjoyable time in the wilds. We talk and laugh about old times, and Callum tells us stories of his village as well. It turns out he's more like us than I originally thought--he was one of the humans who lived in the Carolina Pack's territory and understands what that's like. There's a story there, and I'm curious to know what it is. Has he seen his family since turning into a lycan? Was he supposed to be one of the claimed men and ran away, or was he just unlucky enough to get bit?

"How old were you when you were bitten and taken from your village?" Charlotte asks.

Callum drops his eyes. "Twelve."

"What happened?" Charlotte presses. This is personal, and the energy in the group goes cold.

"I don't want to talk about it." He abruptly picks up his plate and leaves.

Charlotte stares at his back, and her eyes are filled with concern. Maybe she really has changed. The Charlotte I knew wouldn't have cared about another person's feelings so much. "Should I go after him and apologize? I didn't mean to upset him."

Knox snorts. "You really didn't think that asking him how he got bitten would make him upset?"

Her cheeks redden. Knox does have a point. "I guess not. I wasn't thinking. I don't like thinking about that night either. I'm going to talk to him."

She hurries to the medical tent where Callum has disappeared. Laik drops into Callum's abandoned seat, and Wanda takes Charlotte's. Her hair is tied into two wild buns on the top of her head, and her eyes glint with malice.

"I thought you two weren't allowed to talk to each other," she says with a sinister grin.

"Maybe we realized that you guys aren't like the wolves who would kill us for disobedience." I give her a hard glare. "We're friends. No one else here is under any restrictions. Don't you think it's been long enough?"

"No one else came to us straight from the wolf city of their own accord either," Laik adds. His lip curls as he studies us for a long minute. My heart speeds, and I try to keep my surface calm and collected, but I lose courage and drop my face to my plate. "You two don't think we know exactly where you came from? You've been the alpha's pet for some time now, haven't you?"

I jerk my head up, wondering how on earth he knows that, but he's looking at Knox.

"It's not as if I had a choice in the matter," Knox spits out. "I was claimed, remember?"

I'm both relieved and scared. I've allowed myself to get too comfortable among these people, thinking they wouldn't hurt me, but I can see now that was a terrible assumption.

"Doesn't matter. It gives us a reason to doubt your loyalty. Both of you. Talk all you want today because tomorrow everything will be different. We may not be the wolves, but we don't tolerate disobedience either. Every action has a consequence." His gaze lands on me. "Remember that tonight during the full moon."

Wanda cackles, and they both get up and leave.

"What do you suppose that means?" Knox demands. He looks around, and his voice goes low. "Maybe we should run away."

I shake my head. "Whatever it is, it can't be worse than me accidentally killing or biting you out in the wilds."

"I'm the only human here." A trace of panic enters his tone. "How long until Laik decides to do something about it?"

It's what I've feared too, but have been too afraid to say. What if Knox gets bitten tonight? Or worse, what if he gets killed? I want to get him out of here, but I don't know how. I can't forget what Callum said about a lot of bites getting infected. If he gets bitten, he might not survive. "I promise, after I learn to control my lycan, we're not staying here a second longer than we have to."

* * *

Only a few hours later, when the sun is bright and warm in the sky, my body goes cold. Shivering so hard I can barely breathe, I drop the firewood I've been collecting and high-tail it to the women's tent. I'm only wearing a tank top and shorts, and I've got to get into heavier layers of clothing immediately. It rained a lot the first few weeks we were in the wilds, but I was too angry with Ryne to really care about something as trivial as the weather. Now that it's May, and the sun is shining, and the trees are budding bright green leaves, I should be comfortable working outside. In fact, it's rather hot. Everyone has been wearing as little clothing as they can get away with, and I am too, but it's as if all that means nothing now. My body thinks it's the middle of an icy winter storm, and I'm outside without a coat.

This must be the beginning of the renewal.

"Are you okay?" a woman asks. The tent is large and made from thick canvas. There's a crate in the corner where we share clothing. I wish we could keep things as our own, but Laik won't allow it. Once something is cleaned, it goes right in the crate and not back to whoever was last wearing it. That means that the women on laundry duty get first choice, and this gal is one of them. She's currently folding clothes and putting them away. She's enjoying this nice day, oblivious to how cold I feel.

I drop to my knees next to her. "I need a coat."

Her eyebrows furrow, and she looks at me knowingly. "This happens to a lot of us when we first transition," she says, then she puts her hand on my forehead. "You're burning up."

"No." I shake my head, growing frantic. "I'm freezing."

She nods toward my cot. "Honey, you have a fever. Go lie down. I'll grab Callum."

I don't know if she has the authority to let me off my duties for the day, but I don't care. If I can't get a coat, then the pile of my blankets will be even better. I crawl over to the cot and bury myself under the mound of warmth. After a few minutes, my shivers start to settle, and I drift off to sleep.

I go in and out of sleep all afternoon--sometimes because I'm having nightmares and sometimes because Callum is trying to help me. When I'm lost to the darkness, finally asleep without dreams, his hands pat my cheeks.

"Leave me," I say groggily. I've never been more tired, and my body feels like a million pounds. I can't even open my eyes.

But those damned hands keep patting at me. "You're burning up." Callum's voice drifts into my thoughts. "You're too hot. This isn't safe."

I don't answer him.

He starts to shake me. "I either give you medicine, or I carry you down to the creek and dump you in the freezing water. One way or another, I'm bringing this temperature down."

That does it. As I fight to open my eyes, my vision blurs and then clears. Callum is in the tent with me, and so are Charlotte and Laik.

"What's happening?" My voice is hoarse, and tears flood my eyes. I didn't think anything would happen to me until tonight.

"This is normal," Laik says. "You'll be fine."

"Is it though?" Charlotte's voice is more concerned than

I've ever heard from her before. "I got a fever but not like this. She shouldn't be so sick that she's flat on her back. I've helped a few people through their first renewal, and I've never seen this."

"If she's meant to be one of us, then she will be okay," Laik says gruffly. "Either the fever cooks her brain, and we bury her, or she comes out the other end stronger than ever. It's up to the virus to decide. Occasionally people don't make it, and that's natural selection."

Everyone goes silent, and time seems to crawl by. I blink, and Laik is gone.

"Don't listen to him," Callum says softly. "We have medicine for a reason."

I'm not sure if he's talking to me or Charlotte. Does it matter at this point? I'm so tired, my body is covered in sweat, and my brain can't hold a thought. My eyes flutter closed again, but Callum shakes me and forces me to sit up.

"You need to drink this." He presses a little cup to my lips, and a gooey liquid fills my mouth. It tastes bitter and sweet and horrible. I cough, trying to get it out, but Charlotte covers my mouth and stares at me hard.

"We're serious," she says. "We have to get your fever down. You won't be human much longer, and then you'll feel so much better." Her eyes start to water, tears forming. "I won't let you down, I promise."

I want to tell her that she's changed, that I don't hate her anymore, but to speak now would be too difficult. With their help, I manage to swallow the medicine. Then they're making me drink water, and soon I'm plummeting back to sleep.

It's restless and endless, and I'm certain I'm going to die.

Everyone dies. It's part of life. I never thought this would be my time, that I'd go so early, but I should've known this would happen. I never took Callum's herbs to help me through this process, and given everything that's happened in the last year, *I should've seen this coming*. If I'd known, would I have done something different? Yes. I would've gone to see my family. I would've said goodbye to the ones I love. I would've found Ryne and told him exactly how I felt. I would've--

Searing, burning, unimaginable pain slices through my core. I bolt up, wide awake, and a bone-deep scream erupts from within.

CHAPTER 12

My eyes pop open. My first thought, before I even register where I am, is that I'm naked. I'm alone. I'm outside. It's dark and--all thoughts are replaced with blinding pain. My head feels like it's too big for my body, like it's about to burst. I squeeze my eyes shut because I can't stand it.

Keeping my eyes closed, I gingerly reach my hands to my face, but they're stopped by a long snout. I jerk my hands away and scream. Only, it doesn't sound like a scream. It sounds like a howl. The pain that started in my head suddenly radiates through my bones and joints. My sense of hearing is strong, and every crack and pop of my hands and feet and bones are magnified. I groan because I know what's happening, and I still can't believe it.

And the pain... Oh my, the sheer pain of this is too much. It's all I can feel. It's as if every inch of my body has been bitten by a fire ant. I scream out.

Again, another howl.

Miraculously, the pain starts to lessen a little until it's a dull ache. Everything still hurts, but it's manageable. I wait another few moments, and it fades even more. I open my eyes, moaning, and scramble up to my knees. My legs don't bend under me like they should, and I stand instead. I'm so tall. The ground is at least two feet farther away than it should be.

I stare at my hands because I can't stand the thought of looking at the rest of my body. My hands are covered in thick brown fur, which is bothersome, but it's my fingers that really horrify me. They are thick, dark, and curl under, and there is a massive yellow claw at the end of each one.

A hunger forms in my throat, and I feel the need to bite, claw, kill something.

I shrink at the thought. I am not a monster. I've never killed anything in my life, and I'm certainly not going to start now.

But the hunger is raw and dry and demanding. I grip at my throat and then remember my creepy hands, and I drop them, now staring at my wolflike feet. I'm a monster.

Welcome to the pack.

I jerk my head up. I didn't realize the lycan could speak telepathically like the wolf shifters. Nobody told me, or maybe it's a secret the lycan keep. Either way, the monsters are all around me.

So, I'm not alone after all.

They move in at once, forming a tight circle. We're somewhere in the woods in a small clearing, and the bright moon hangs overhead, a light in the darkness. There are thick trees beyond the lycan, but here the ground is grassy and damp. And it's just us. I have nowhere to run.

How do you feel? That voice is different from the first, and I can recognize it, but not completely. Callum perhaps.

"Not . . ." But my voice doesn't come out. It's more like a strangled cry.

You have to speak to us through your mind. It's okay, go ahead. Has the pain gone away?

I can't be sure who is talking at this point. The sounds aren't the same as human sounds, and the thoughts come at me against my will. I'm not part of this pack so lycan must be able to communicate to any other lycan. It's not like the wolves, where they're so connected through their links they can anticipate each other's moves. But still, it's eerie.

Answer the question, another voice cuts in uninvited.

I shake my head, and shaggy fur falls into my eyes.

A large lycan steps out from the circle, and the rest close in so there are no gaps. At least they are keeping me here instead of letting me run wild and hurt someone. The need to feed is growing stronger every second. It's getting harder and harder to focus on anything else. I've never been this hungry before. I didn't even know it was possible.

The massive lycan stands in front of me, at least three feet taller and twice as wide as my monster. His stance radiates dominance, and I keep my eyes plastered to the ground. He takes a giant paw with gnarled fingers and forces my snout up to look at him.

I am your alpha. Pledge your allegiance.

This must be Laik.

Is giving him what he wants the best thing to do? I don't know this man very well, and I certainly don't know what his plans are. So far, he's done nothing to show me that he's trustworthy. I didn't even know that the lycan had alphas until now. The fact that they have alphas at all is unsettling. And they can communicate telepathically? That would allow them to be far more organized than I realized. I stare at this man, this creature who I want nothing to do with, and gather my courage.

No.

He howls, and I jerk back, the sound filling me with fear. It was the same sound that came every full moon and stole away our friends.

Why not? he bellows.

Because I don't know you. I don't know this. I hold up my paw, surprised at how clear my thoughts are. He inches closer, and I'm hit with an overwhelming fear of what he could do to me in this form. My fight or flight instinct so badly wants to kick in but either choice could end up with me dead. *Let me have a few moons to understand what I am before joining your pack.*

He bares his teeth, and I'm certain he's about to attack, but instead, he steps away. *I thought you might feel that way. It's a shame, but perhaps after tonight, you'll feel differently about what it means to disobey me.*

I'm waiting for the punchline. I know it's coming.

Enjoy your meal.

He goes back to his place in the circle, and I can't figure out what he means, but I am hungry. So, so hungry.

All at once, they howl, and I stumble back, tripping over something.

I land flat on my back, but it doesn't hurt like it should. I shake it off and scramble onto all fours. There is no more pain, only raw unfiltered hunger. I'm desperate for something, anything to feed on. I smell it before I see it--warm, savory, and begging to be mine. But when I locate the object of the smell, horror fills my chest. Lying right beneath my snout, hands and feet tied up and mouth gagged, is Knox.

The lycans howl once again. As a human, their howling was chaotic screeching to my ears and nothing more. But now, something about the howls call to me, luring me into a trance. The hunger keeps growing, and I force myself to step away from Knox. I want to give in. I want to feed. But I can't do that to Knox. Not my first love. Not him.

The hunger claws at my stomach, a beast tearing me apart from the inside out.

No, I scream through the telepathic link, *I won't touch him.*

Are you sure? Wanda's voice snaps back. *We saved him just for you.*

Saliva drips down my jaw, matting my fur. It would be so easy. Knox lies there, eyes wide, shaking his head back and forth. I wish I could talk to him, tell him this isn't my fault. I would never willingly choose this, but now that I'm here, I don't know how I can resist. My choices were stripped away from me too.

I just wish I could ask him to forgive me.

My thoughts melt away, and the hunger takes control, his human scent filling my nostrils. Saliva pools in my mouth, and I open it, the spit rolling out and dripping on Knox. I snap my jaws shut. The desire to bite him is all-consuming, and soon I can't remember why I wouldn't want to.

I shake my head again. I can't hurt Knox. I reach my hand out to untie the rope that binds his feet, but instead my claw rips open his skin, the blood pouring out. He bellows, but it's muffled by his gag.

I try to clear my nostrils of the scent of his blood, but it's useless. Every cell in my body wants to bite.

Bite. Bite. Bite.

The chant fills my brain, and I glance around. Each and every monster in the circle is watching me with intensity, stomping their feet to the rhythm of the chant in my head.

Bite. Bite. Bite.

But I don't want to. This is Knox. I can't hurt him.

I run to the edge of the circle, needing to get away from Knox, but rough paws and snapping jaws shove me back toward him.

The warm salty smell of his blood calls to me, and for a moment my mind clears. Why is that? Before the last world war killed them off, vampires were the bloodsuckers. But now, here I am, here we are, no better.

As quickly as the thoughts come, they leave, replaced by fantasies of sinking my fangs into Knox's flesh and tasting that sweet blood. I lunge, and then I bite, and then I'm lost to the bliss of his flesh.

CHAPTER 13

I bolt awake to the morning sun. My memories are hazy, and my bones ache, but at least I'm not burning up anymore. The fever is long gone, but there is a stench around me that makes me gag.

I roll over with a groan and press my face into the dewy grass. *What happened last night?* I'm naked, and my head is pounding. I stand, trying to shake off the weakness in my limbs. I brush myself off, searching for something to tell me where I am. I'm back to my human form, but that's almost worse. Because my hands and legs and everything are covered in blood.

The night resurfaces in my mind like a slingshot and I cry out in horror. What have I done to Knox? I stare at my hands. *No.*

I crumple to my knees, overcome with sobs. As much as I want to think last night didn't happen, it did. It was real. The memories come in flashes. The way his flesh felt in my teeth. The blood spurting around my jaw. His horrified scream. After that, the memory is gone, but I know it happened, and I'll never forget what I've done.

I killed Knox--they made me kill him. There's no other explanation for all the blood. I don't know exactly how it all happened, but I did lunge for him. And that was my decision. I wasn't strong enough to resist the hunger.

My grief gives way to rage, and I jump up, tearing through the forest. I'm barefoot and naked as the day I was born, but right now I couldn't care less. As soon as I find the camp, I'm going to kill Laik. He is responsible for this! He punished me by making me kill the one person who he knew I had left in this miserable world. And for what? Because I wouldn't instantly join his stupid pack? Or was it because Knox and I defied him by talking? *Talking!* I don't care that he's bigger than me or that he's the alpha of this ramshackle encampment. He set me up, and he has to pay for what he did.

My senses are stronger, and my body is faster as I maneuver through the brush with ease. When I catch the smell of something cooking on a fire, I head in that direction. Someone's making eggs for breakfast, which is considered a treat out here. I'm not hungry. I don't know if I'll ever be hungry after what I did last night. It's sick to even think about. As I catch sight of a trail of smoke twirling up into the morning sky, someone tackles me to the ground.

I growl and lash out, my fist colliding with a jaw. "Get off me!"

"Relax," Charlotte growls back. "I'm trying to help you."

I roll off her and stand. She's already clothed and is rubbing her jaw. She glances at the ground and points to the clothes that are now scattered around us. "I brought these for you."

I glare, but I gather up the clothes. I turn so my back is toward her and hurry to dress, suddenly feeling awkward. I've never really been naked around anyone before. My hands shake as I slip on my shirt, my mind still on Knox and what I did. When my feet miss the hole of the pants, I trip and fall. And then I start crying.

"Hey, it's okay," she says, sitting next to me.

"No. It's not." I finish up sliding into the pants, ready to go find Laik, but the tears won't stop. They burn trails of anger down my cheeks. "I have every right to cry after what you guys did to me." My voice cracks. "And to Knox."

The forest grows silent as we sit there. She doesn't know what to say, and I don't either. I wonder if she was there last night, watching me devour my friend. And suddenly, I hate her. Because I understand her now, I'm no better than she is. I'm a murderer, and I don't think I can survive with the knowledge of what I've done.

"Finish getting dressed," she says softly. "Last night was not what you think it was. I have something to show you."

I snort. Not what I think it was? I remember tearing into Knox's flesh. There is no other way to interpret what I did.

I follow her, not because I want to, but because I know she'll lead me back to Laik, and I can kill him for what he did to me. Then I'm going to find out who else was in that circle and hunt them down. They will all pay for forcing me to kill my friend. I'll never forgive myself, but maybe revenge will help me survive this.

I hate that I'm more like Charlotte than I thought I was.

I should've taken Knox and gotten out of that situation, found shelter somewhere else, or at the very least, set him free. I could have. He even suggested it yesterday. The other lycans didn't open my jaws and make me bite. I did that all on my own, and now it's too late.

We stride into the encampment, and I'm ready to raise hell. There's not a stream near this one, but there's been so much rain that we've collected it in big bins, using filters supplied by the panthers to keep our source clean. Several of the people are using that water to wash the lycan stench off. I should want to, but I'm more bent on revenge. I look around for Laik, but I don't see him yet. There are more lycan in the camp than there had been in the circle last night, and as I glance around, I wonder who was there. Who watched me murder another soul? Who treated my first renewal like a sport? It's sick.

Charlotte pushes me toward the medic tent. "Go on in."

"I don't want to see Callum right now," I snap angrily.

"I heard that," Callum calls from the inside. "Now get in here."

I pull the tent flap back. Callum hovers over someone, wiping their brow with a cloth. Apparently, I'm not the only one who had a rough night.

"I'm not sick. I don't know why . . ." My words die off when Callum moves off to the side.

Knox lies there, still and pale and unmoving.

I drop to my knees and cry out. "Why would you show me this?" I swivel my head so I don't have to look at him.

Charlotte points. "Because he's not dead."

"What?" Turning so fast that I nearly fall over, I crawl to the bed. His chest rises and falls a tiny bit with his breath.

Tears of relief stream down my face, and I reach for his hand, but he's still unconscious, so it hangs limp and cold in mine.

"You bit him," Charlotte says, joining us. "But it's not your fault." She points to his bare chest, where an angry red welt is rising.

"Laik was going to bite him if you didn't," Callum adds. "It was inevitable."

I find my voice. "That still doesn't make this okay."

I stare at my friend's beautifully broken face. It's scratched up, swollen, and there's a bruise on his cheek. I bring his cold hand to my cheek and just watch him, afraid that at any moment he's going to die on me. My body is tired, and I really should go wash up, but I'm not leaving until Knox wakes.

He's going to be angry with me. I just turned him into a monster, but at least he's alive.

Charlotte and Callum whisper behind me. I ignore them. It doesn't matter what they have to say to me now. Knox is alive, and I'm going to do whatever it takes to keep him that way.

"Poppy, let's go wash up," Charlotte says, laying a hand on my shoulder.

"No. I'm staying right here."

Callum chuckles. "No offense, but you stink. I'll stay here with him. When he wakes, you don't want him passing out again from the stench, do you?"

He has a point, but I'm still reluctant to go. "Were you there last night?" I ask, eyeing him with mistrust.

"Where?"

"In the circle with Laik."

He shakes his head adamantly. "No. I didn't even know what he planned to do. Charlotte and I found out this morning when they returned."

"I was so pissed when he brought you outside without me," Charlotte says. "I wanted to be there to help you, but after you passed out, Laik and a few others took you. They told us if we followed, we'd be dead meat."

I don't know if I believe them, but I want to. I need someone on my side here. I decide their story is good enough for me. If they weren't there, then they aren't the enemy.

"Okay, I'm going to wash up right outside the tent. If anything changes with him at all, you call for me."

"We'll be right here waiting for you," Callum says.

I step back out into the muggy air and find a bin of water. There are clean rags next to it, and I dip one in and start to clean off the lycan stench. I keep my eyes peeled for Laik, but I don't see him anywhere.

Guilt still crawls through my insides, but at least Knox is still alive. He'll become a monster, but he'll get to live a full life. Even though I hate the lycan that lives inside of me, I'd rather have it than be dead.

I rush through the washing and then hurry back into the tent. Knox still lies there just like he did before. Callum stands and lets me take his place. Charlotte rests in the corner, her gaze watchful and alert. She looks just as worried as I do. I'm not surprised, she's always had a thing for Knox. Callum kneels next to me, placing a gentle hand on my back.

"He's going to be okay. He just had a rough night."

Okay? Being bitten by a lycan is never okay. "What if he hates me?" I ask with a small voice.

"He won't. He loves you," Charlotte says. "He told me that you wouldn't give him a second chance. He's been whining about it ever since I joined up with you guys."

I ignore the obvious irritation in her voice. "Look what I did to him." I run my fingers along the angry welt on his chest.

"I told you before, if you hadn't, Laik would've," Callum argues. "It was inevitable. Don't you wonder why Knox wasn't taken to the panther city straight away? Laik doesn't take care of someone for no reason."

"But why not let Knox be human? He wasn't hurting anything. Laik didn't need another lycan. He's worse than the wolves."

Charlotte shakes her head, suddenly defensive. "No way. He's not enslaving women." Her change in tone catches me off guard.

"But he still made me turn Knox. That's cruel."

Charlotte scoffs. "But it's not worse than what the wolf shifters are doing."

"What did Knox ever do to Laik?" I press.

"He's that wolf alpha's lackey, which makes him far from innocent," Laik barks from behind me as he steps into the tent. I whip around to face my newest enemy.

CHAPTER 14

"If you cause trouble," Laik says, towering over me, "I will enjoy putting you in your place, but you won't like it. You may even end up in the medic tent next to your little friend."

But he doesn't know what I'm fully capable of. He never let me join his guards, stating he couldn't trust me yet. I use his underestimation of me to my advantage and whip out a leg, kicking him in the shin. When he looks down, I punch him square in the face, and he tumbles out of the tent onto his back.

"You sure about that, old man?" I ask, following.

Now it's me who's towering over him, every bit of anger I've felt over the last month on display for the whole camp to see. Blood drips from his nostrils and into his mouth, making his teeth pink when he smiles. And then he laughs, a manic sound that sends a shiver through my body. "Don't say I didn't warn you, little girl."

He dives for me, taking me around the middle and flattening me on my back. He's a huge man, but he's not as big as the wolf shifters, and I trained with them for months. I can do this. My mind goes clear, and my attention zeroes in on what I'm about to do. I've never killed anyone before, but I'm willing to kill him for what he's done. If this pack works anything like the wolves, that will make me the alpha. I'll be able to make some decisions around here and finally be let in on all the nitty-gritty secrets.

He rolls over and pushes me off him with so much force that I go flying back. I'm quick to recover, and then we're both up on our feet. The rest of the camp has realized what's going on, and they run over. When a couple of them go for me, Laik yells at them to stop. "She's mine." His chuckle is low. "Let's see what she's got."

"My pleasure." I go for him again, this time aiming to knee him between the legs. I will play as dirty as I have to in order to win this fight. As far as I'm concerned, anything goes, but I miss, and he clocks me on the back of the head. My vision blurs for a second, and I drop to my knees.

Breathe, I tell myself. *Just breathe.*

"I should kill you for what you did last night," Laik says against my ear.

"Are you kidding me?" I gasp. "I didn't do anything."

"You refused to recognize me as your alpha. You embarrassed me in front of my pack, and you're doing it again." And then his meaty arm is around my neck, and he's pulling tight. My oxygen is cut off, and I have limited time. The people are wildly chanting his name. They're angry that I didn't accept him. They must see it as though I rejected everyone here, but that's not it--if only they realized how deranged their leader really is, surely they wouldn't follow him.

I don't simply claw and bite and kick and punch. I use my skills to gain control of the situation by twisting from his hold and breaking free. He comes for me again, but this time I know what I'm looking for and create space between us at the perfect moment. Catching him off guard, I lock him in a chokehold of my own. I've got one arm around his neck, compressing his esophagus, and my other arm is locked to secure the hold. I squeeze as tight as I can, my muscles burning with the effort. If he wasn't so big, I'd be able to stay this way until he passes out, but the man is a beast, and he rips from me after a few short seconds.

"You're going to regret that," he snarls, knocking me down and sitting on my chest. He shifts a leg to press down on my neck, and once again, I can't breathe. I fight with everything I have, but it's no use. He's just so much bigger and stronger than me. Impossibly strong. Even more so than the wolves, despite being the size of a human. I realize why as the world begins to fade away. It's because of the moon--lycan are strongest around the full moons and weakest at the new moons. Of all the times I could've chosen to fight Laik, this was possibly the worst.

But I'm a lycan too.

I'm stronger now, and I can't give up.

With all the strength I have left, I twist around. I'm on my stomach now, and he's still on top of me, but I have more space to breathe. I suck in a deep breath, and then I rear my head back, slamming it into his nose. It cracks, and he bellows, dropping his weight off me for just a moment, but it's enough for me to scramble away. I'm back on my feet in an instant, ready for round three, when he jumps up and glares at me. Blood streams down his face, and a sick sense of satisfaction fills me. If I hadn't broken it before, there's no doubt I just finished the job. I fist my hands and bare my teeth, something primal taking over me. I'm ready to fight this man to the death. There isn't an ounce of fear left in my body. No matter what happens next, I have to try.

"Stop!" A familiar voice cuts through the crowd, and I turn to find Knox. He's barely standing, hanging off of Charlotte's arm. He looks terrible, but at least he's awake. "Both of you, just stop."

"I'm doing this for you," I snap back. "I never would've bitten you if it wasn't for him."

"You don't understand, Poppy. I asked to be bitten. I wanted this." Knox's face twists in pain as he stands taller. I blink at him, stunned. Why would anyone want to be a lycan? It doesn't make sense. "I've thought about it all month, and when the moon came, and they took you away for your renewal, I asked Laik to bite me. I didn't know they were going to tie me up and throw me to a new lycan though." He glares at Laik, and Wanda laughs maniacally.

"He's right." Laik mops the blood up with his shirt and smiles down at me smugly. "He wants to be stronger. Can't say I blame him."

"She could've killed me." Knox gives him a nasty look. "Don't act like what you did was okay."

He's right. It wasn't okay, and it will never be okay, but asking to become a lycan?

"There are consequences to your actions out here." Laik speaks loud enough for everyone to hear. "You should all use this as a lesson. Poppy and Knox were told not to speak to each other, and they broke that instruction. So really"—he pauses to scowl at Knox—"you did this to yourself. And I missed the part where you said thank you." Silence falls over the group, and Laik repeats himself. "I said I missed the part where you said thank you."

"Thank you," Knox mumbles.

I'm rooted in place, stunned by what just happened. Knox wants to be a lycan? Why would he do that to himself? I don't understand how Knox could want a life at the mercy of the moon's phases. He knows how dangerous lycans are and the horrible things they can do. Was he really so frustrated that he'd resort to something drastic like this?

"He wanted to be stronger," Laik says, as if reading my mind, "but he also wanted to prove his loyalty to us. Something you have yet to do."

"What do you want from me?" I growl. I could fight him again, but the wind has been taken from my sails, and I'm suddenly weary. "Don't you think I've been through enough?"

"You didn't submit to me as your alpha, so in exchange, you're going to have to do something for me." He pauses, letting my curiosity eat me up. But I don't ask. I know he's going to keep talking. I thought the man was quiet when I first met him, but now I think it's the opposite. He loves to hear himself talk. "We're going to the wolf city tomorrow night for a little . . . mission. And you, dear Poppy, are coming with us."

CHAPTER 15

My mind reels with the implications of Laik's declaration. *I could see Ryne again.* Do I want that? Of course I do, but I also want to break his nose like I just broke Laik's. He betrayed me, and I don't know if I love him or hate him. Maybe it'll always be both.

Callum touches my arm. "Go help Knox back to his tent. I'll take care of Laik's nose. It'll heal easily, but I need to reset it first."

I glare over at Laik, where he's mopping up his bloody nose with his shirt. He seems amused by this whole thing, and it makes me want to scream. "Am I allowed to talk to Knox now or not?"

He drops his soiled shirt, crosses his arms, and smirks. "Sure, you can talk to him, but remember the price you paid for that luxury last time."

I want to stay and argue or fight or something, but at this point, I don't think it will do any good.

Charlotte holds tight to Knox's left arm. I take his right,

and he hobbles back to his tent. Once there, we gently guide him down to his bed, and he collapses onto it, breathing hard. He slowly scoots himself back to the wall.

I sit on his bed across from him, and Charlotte perches on the edge.

Knox looks back and forth between us. "Charlotte, I need you to leave us alone."

"But . . . but . . . I helped you. Don't shut me out now."

He reaches over and grabs her hand. Something about the gesture is intimate, and I'm not sure how to feel about that. I don't want Knox for myself, but I don't trust Charlotte either. Then again, maybe I shouldn't trust anyone at this point.

"I know," he says to her. "But Poppy and I have had no alone time since we arrived at the camp, and there are things we need to discuss."

"Things you don't want me to know about?" Charlotte asks, hurt lacing her words.

Knox swallows. "Please just leave us alone. I'll talk to you later."

She stands, glaring at me, and then storms from the tent. Funny how she takes her anger with Knox out on me. Some things never change.

I give Knox a knowing grin. "She's pouty today, isn't she?"

Knox nods, wincing. "She and I became pretty close while you and I weren't able to talk. I think she liked having me to herself."

I nudge his foot and give him my brightest smile. "Can't say I blame her." I want to keep the mood light because I feel like it's about to get very heavy.

Knox frowns. "Don't do that, Poppy,"

"Do what?"

"Pretend like you like me," he says abruptly. "I think after everything we've been through, you owe me the courtesy of not leading me on."

"I'm not. I just . . . You're my friend."

"That's the thing, Poppy. I don't want to just be your friend."

"I know. But I can't ignore my own feelings. My heart belongs to someone else."

He sighs and rubs a hand along his face. "Fine. But please don't give me hope where there is none."

"I understand."

"But that's not what I wanted to talk to you about. You deserve to know why I chose to become lycan and what they have on me."

"Come on, Knox, they can't have anything on you."

"Do you know why Ryne trusted me so much?"

I shake my head.

He stares down at his hands. "The night of my claiming, Ryne and his betas came to visit all the claimed boys after the festival. It was quite late and still dark. There were only three of us. While they were laying down the law--no touching any of the girls and stuff--we were attacked by a group of lycan."

I bite my lip and let that sink in. It seems like the lycan have been going after the city nearly every full moon for a while. "What happened?"

He shrugs. "I hid like a coward. They got away with the other two boys, and Ryne's betas ran after them, leaving

Ryne behind alone. Then, out of nowhere, three more lycan attacked Ryne."

He pauses, and his face screws up like he's remembering everything. "The wolves are quite well armed on the full moons. They can shift, but they also have swords and knives to fight with--I know now that those are for the beta wives to protect themselves and their kin." A haunted sheen passes over his eyes. "I was hiding between two cars, and at my feet was a long sword that someone had left behind. I'd never wielded one in my life, but my brothers and I used to play with sticks, pretending we were fighting with swords. I didn't know at that time how brutal the wolves were, just all the stories we'd heard about the lycan. So, as Ryne was fighting the three lycan, I attacked them from behind, killing two. I can see now that I got lucky because there's no way I would've been successful if I hadn't snuck up on them. The third one ran away."

"You saved Ryne's life," I whisper. No wonder Ryne trusted Knox so much. What claimed person would risk their life to save their captor? It must've taken loads of courage.

"I did." He says the words like he regrets his actions.

"If you hadn't, Anders would be alpha, and you and I both know he's worse than Ryne. Knox, I'm so proud of you."

He shakes his head. "Well, it turns out that the lycan who got away was Laik."

No wonder Laik didn't trust us. We're lucky he didn't kill Knox on sight, but that explains how he knew our first story about running away from a village was a lie.

"When did you find out that Laik knew about you?"

"Yesterday, the son of a bitch kept his secret to himself until he could use it against me."

My mouth pops open. "So what did he do?"

"Well, while you were in your tent with a fever, he came to me and told me the whole story. I was backed into a corner. I told him how much I regretted protecting Ryne, and that from that day on I've been seeking a way to atone because over the last year I've seen firsthand how brutal the wolves are." His voice goes low. "He wasn't buying it, wanted to use me against you as punishment for killing two of his men, so I told him how much I wanted to become lycan. I pledged myself to his cause, to kill Ryne and the other wolves."

My heart splinters for him. "So you didn't really want to become lycan?"

"No," he whispers bitterly. "But I did ask him to do it. I couldn't see any way out. But there is an upside to this."

"What's that?" I can't see how there could be an upside to being a monster. I'd do anything to reverse what I've become.

"I can kill wolves now, and I wasn't lying when I said I wanted Ryne dead. I want them all dead."

"You can't mean that." My voice is soft, but I don't feel soft at all. I feel hard. Defensive.

"I do. Poppy, they kidnap innocent men and women and do horrific things to them. The more time I spend here with the lycan, the more I realize how wrong everything is. The lycan don't attack our villages. The wolves just make it seem like they do. The lycan are the good guys, not the wolves."

"You honestly believe Laik is a good guy?" I roll my eyes. I can't believe what I'm hearing.

"He's better than Ryne." Again, he sounds so bitter and angry. I'm angry at Ryne too, but to want him dead? I could never . . .

I stand. "You're wrong."

And I march from the tent. I can't have this conversation anymore because the awful thing is, I think he might be right.

* * *

"Nobody is telling you anything," Wanda says, "so don't ask."

"Wasn't gonna," I grumble and haul myself up into the back of the truck.

"Behave yourselves," Laik adds.

Two other lycan I don't know very well--Tanner and Christian--load into the back. They settle down across from me, giving me horrible looks. I'm not surprised. There's no shortage of animosity toward me since I haven't accepted their alpha as my own.

"You have to put this on." Laik leans over the edge of the truck, a red bandana clutched in his meaty hand. "I don't want you knowing where we are and how to get back here. I still don't trust you."

I sigh heavily but don't protest because I already know the man isn't going to budge on this. And honestly, I can't say I blame him. If I were in his position, I would treat me with trepidation too. But I still don't trust him, especially after the stunt he pulled with Knox.

He ties the fabric tightly around my face, and everything goes dark. I'm never going to take him as my alpha, never going to officially join this strange pack, but he doesn't have to know that. The least I can do is follow through with whatever mission he has in mind and hope it's something that helps my friends back in the city. If what he said about helping humans is true, then this mission should be an easy one for me to accept.

The truck engine rumbles to life, and we're off. The metal of the truck bed had been so uncomfortable when we drove across the war-torn roads to the panther city, but it doesn't bother me anymore. It's as if turning into a lycan has made me immune to pain. At least, right now, I feel amazing, but I'm pretty sure that will change with the waxing and waning of the moon. What will I feel like in a couple of weeks when the sky is empty again? My only hope is that I won't feel worse than I did as a human. I doubt I'll be so lucky.

Tanner speaks up over the sound of the engine. "If you don't do a good job today, then you'll be tossed out on your ass and will have to fend for yourself. The wilds aren't a safe place for a little girl like you, Poppy."

Is that true though? I haven't had a chance to find out. If anything, I'll go to the panther city and ask for help. I'm pretty sure I can find my way there.

"Yeah," Christian adds in a gravelly voice. "Think about all those lone wolves. You know, the ones that your wolf city kicks out. Ever wonder what happens to them?"

Of course I've wondered about them, but I hadn't thought to ask. Now I'm interested. "Where do they go?"

"Well, most of them aren't given asylum in the panther

territory. You know the wolves and the panthers are enemies, right? They have to plead their case to the panthers to be taken in and most won't take that risk. Either that or they're too proud. So what can they do but try to survive? They're out there in the forest, living on scraps and lonely for companionship. Can you imagine what one of them would do if they found a woman alone?"

I swallow hard because I can imagine, and it's not good. "I want to prove myself to your people and to Laik," I say, and I'm not entirely lying. I need safety and security. I need answers. And I need help. I don't want to kill Ryne, but I want to let him know exactly how I feel about what he did to me and my friends. I'm aching to see Joanna, but I fear I never will. And I'm sure that Abi is lost to the mating houses by now. I hope they're both still alive, and that I can make things right for them somehow.

"We'll see if you're being honest soon enough."

The truck stops, and thankfully, the blindfold is removed. I blink, taking in the brightness of the evening sunset. It paints swashes of orange and red across my vision. Then the trees come into focus. And then the people.

We're not alone.

CHAPTER 16

I climb out of the truck with the others. I want to fold in on myself, guard myself from these new faces. There are about thirty in all, but I can't trust them. I don't think I'll trust any new person ever again. The need to run away is powerful, but I force myself to keep my arms at my sides, my shoulders square, and my head up. I need to be seen as strong.

"Welcome to the Resistance." Laik pats me on the back. "Don't embarrass me."

I barely register his words because standing across from me are two people I'd given up hope on ever seeing again. A little squeal of disbelief escapes my throat, and I nearly crumple to my knees. I'm propelled forward and into the arms of Joanna.

"Poppy!" she says into my hair as she hugs me. "You're here! What are you doing here?" She steps back, and her eyebrows crease as she studies me.

Grady gives me a look up and down, scanning me too.

He doesn't exactly look happy to see me, or maybe he's unhappy because of the arm that's now a scarred-over stump above his elbow. "She's a lycan," he says. "I can smell it on her."

Joanna's face falls. "You got bit?"

Tears spring to my eyes. "The night of the festival, right after you guys left."

"You mean after you saved our lives," Grady says. He nods in appreciation but still keeps his distance. I'm just grateful he's alive.

Joanna hugs me again and whispers in my ear. "Don't mind him. It's in his nature to hate lycan, but we're both so grateful for what you did."

I know she's right, but his attitude kind of hurts. I don't feel what Grady feels. There's no inner need to not want to be around him. But as I step back, I take in the alarming fact that I'm the only lycan who feels that way. The rest of them are keeping their distance from Grady. Either there's a bias that they've learned, or something is wrong with me. I'm glad for it though. I could never hate Grady. And I don't hate all the wolves. People should be judged on their actions--and not the ones beyond their control. This ideology either makes me foolish, or it makes me wise. I haven't decided which yet.

I just hope that Grady isn't in danger here.

"Let's get started," a woman speaks up. I would know that voice anywhere. I turn around to find Madame Delphine at the head of the group. I gape at her, but she gives me a curt nod and nothing more. She's all business, here to do a job, and nothing is slowing her down. "We have limited time."

I peer around at the group and realize there's a mix of lycans and humans here. Madame Delphine obviously came from the wolf city, but I don't know about the others. Nobody else is familiar to me.

I stay close to Joanna, and Laik takes his place right next to me. "Who's your wolf friend?" he asks, motioning toward Grady. His tone is steady, but his eyes are distrustful.

"Grady. Ryne nearly killed him." I point to Grady's missing arm. "He's not part of that pack anymore."

That makes him a lone wolf, but he's got Joanna, so I know he'll never be alone, and that makes me feel slightly better about everything that went down. Laik gives Grady a stiff nod, but before anything more can be said, Madame Delphine continues her speech.

"Our mission tonight is to rescue Elle. She's been forced into a marriage that she didn't want with a man who is more cruel than I ever imagined." My heart tightens, and I find it odd that she would speak of her son in that way. I thought they were close. Maybe Thorn got to him though, and he's changed. Or maybe I didn't know him all that well in the first place, and he's always been like that. "She's taken up residence in the alpha's house, but we aren't sure exactly where. As we speak, the wolves are being lured away from the house, so you should be able to easily get her."

Her eyes roam over the group and then meet mine. She gives me a sad, regretful smile. Does she feel responsible for what's happened to me? Part of me wants to be angry with her for not preparing me better, or at least not bringing me into the Resistance while I was still at Drayton

Hall, but she's easy to forgive. The woman has faced as many hardships in her life as I have, if not more. Our eyes stay locked for a long moment, as if a whole conversation is passing between us, and then she turns to find Grady.

"Everybody, this is Grady. He is one of the wolves we can count on, and I expect you all to treat him the same as you would any other member of our resistance." There are mumbles of approval and dissent, which she quickly cuts off. "Grady, you know how to get to the alpha's house and how to get in and out, so I want you to lead this mission. When it's over, please send me word as to the success or failure of Elle's rescue."

Grady inclines his head and weaves his way to the front of the group. Madame Delphine gives him a hug, tugs her hood over her head, and quietly slips away. I wish I could follow after her, to get information about what's been happening back in the city and with the other claimed girls. I want to know what Ryne has been up to, where Thorn is, and if Abi is okay. There are so many questions spinning in my head, but I'm certain she has to get back. I wonder what Thorn would do to her if he found out she was in charge of the Resistance. Perhaps she was just a messenger, but everyone listened to her, so whatever she is must be high up.

That makes me smile. One of the highest leaders--if not the highest--is King Thorn's old beta wife and the mother of Ryne. How's that for irony? It goes to show that the cunning of a wronged woman shouldn't be underestimated.

Grady looks around at our group, making eye contact with everyone. "We're going to split into four groups. If we go into the city all at once, we'll attract too much attention. One group will stay here to keep watch, one will go into the alpha's house, and the two others will be placed on our path to and from the house to offer reinforcements as needed. I will lead the group into the house. I need three others to volunteer as group leaders."

Three men raise their hands. Grady splits us up into groups, putting me, two other men, and one woman with him and Joanna. I'm the only lycan in his group.

"I go with Poppy," Laik says from behind me.

"I'm Laik." He puffs out his chest and glares. "Poppy is new to my pack. I need to keep an eye on her. She doesn't go anywhere without me."

I roll my eyes because I'm not okay with this, but I know better than to challenge Laik right now. We need to be focused on helping Elle, and he's the kind of man to let his ego get in the way of the mission.

Grady stares at him for a moment, looking like he wants to argue, but just sighs instead. "James, switch places with Laik."

We all split up and head toward the city on foot. Grady leads, and Joanna loops her arm through mine as we fall to the back of the group. Laik stays near the front with Grady. Grady's movements are stiff, but he seems to be carrying on a conversation with Laik. I wonder if Laik is trying to push Grady for information about me, or maybe it's the other way around. Does Grady still trust me? Or has everything changed now that I've succumbed to lycanthropy?

"It's so good to see you," Joanna says, nudging me in

that familiar way of hers, "but I'm sorry you were bitten. What happened?"

The weight of keeping it a secret breaks. "In the chaos after you left, the lycan attacked," I whisper softly. "I got caught in the crossfire. Instead of killing me, Ryne took me to the edge of the city and banished me."

Her eyes widen and shine with tears. "If I had known, I would've taken you with us. You shouldn't have been alone. I bet you were so scared."

"I was scared, but I wasn't alone." I squeeze her hand. "He sent Knox with me."

"Knox?"

"You know, Ryne's driver." I hate that Knox was so irrelevant that she didn't know his name. He'll never be irrelevant to me.

"Oh, yeah, him. Why did he send him with you?"

"Ryne trusted him to help me, I think." I don't add that Knox and I knew each other before. It feels like a lifetime ago and no longer relevant, but really, I just don't want Joanna to question me. I kept Knox a secret from her, and I shouldn't have, but it's something I don't know how to explain after everything we've been through. "It only took one day for a lycan pack to find us." I eye the back of Laik's head warily. "I'm still not sure about them, but they helped me through my first renewal."

If help is what you would call it. I'll never forgive Laik for what he did to me and Knox that night.

"Renewal?"

"It's what they call turning into a lycan."

"Was it scary?"

I nod. "And painful."

She squeezes my arm a little tighter. "I'm so sorry."

I shrug. "It's okay. I'm surviving."

A shadow passes over her face. "Us too." There's something in her voice that tells me she's not fully okay. Maybe she's just scared, but the Joanna I know doesn't get scared easily. There's something more going on here.

"Where are you guys living?" Would it be possible to abandon Laik and join her and Grady instead? It might still be hard, but at least I'd be with people I trust and who actually care about me. I'd want Knox to come with us as well, but since he's been bitten, he'll need a group of lycan to help him through his first renewal.

"We're staying near the outskirts of the panther city with another resistance camp." She swallows hard. "It was pretty scary when we first got out. Grady almost bled to death, and then we had to find a way to get me safely through the radiation field." She smiles softly. "But we did it, somehow. Thanks to you, Poppy. We'd both be dead if it hadn't been for what you and Abi did for us."

Thinking about Abi makes my heart hurt. I hope she's okay, but I know she probably isn't. I failed her and will never forgive myself for it. When I got bit, and Ryne rushed me away from the battle, I should've demanded we retrieve Abi first. But I'd been consumed in my own pain and fear, and I selfishly left her behind. Now I'm sure it's too late.

"Can I come back with you? I don't want to go back to the lycan camp." My voice drops another octave. "They're so rough, and their alpha isn't my favorite person." I hate what he made me do to Knox, and I don't respect the group at all.

She shakes her head. "No lycan are allowed. I'm sorry."

I let out a breath, wondering if she's staying with humans or banished wolves or both. "It's okay. But I want to see you more often. I miss you."

"Me too."

Laik is just going to have to learn to trust me. I won't pledge myself to his pack, and I want the freedom to come and go. If he won't let me do it, then I'll just find a way to get into the panther city. Charlotte did it. I can too. It might have to wait until after Knox gets control of his lycan though.

She smiles, but there's something in her eyes that I've never seen there before, something I can't quite place. Regret? Fear?

Wolves patrol the city, and we go quiet the closer we get. I keep imagining that we're going to be found out and attacked at any moment. I have a knife to protect me, and I'm strong from the recent full moon, but that's it. I doubt it's enough to fight off a wolf. We move quickly, methodically, and ever so carefully. Since there's not a full moon tonight, I hope the wolves have their guard down a little. They may not know that even though we can't shift we're still strong, the moon's illumination favoring us. Maybe we can really do this.

"We have to cross the river to get to the city," Grady says. "The best way to do that will be to go over the bridge."

My heart lurches because I've seen that bridge and know it's falling apart. There's no way it's safe, but maybe it's better than trying to go by boat. Boats aren't always the quietest, and I know the docks near the betas are all heavily guarded.

We are exposed, running from the cropping of trees to the bridge, and just because it's night doesn't make it safe. Shifters can see in the dark when they're in their wolf forms, and the moon is bright enough to reveal us to anyone who could happen to look our way. A shiver runs up my spine as we get to the bridge. It's riddled with gaping holes, and the concrete is crumbling in places.

"Hang onto the rails, and no more talking," Grady instructs.

We follow, me right behind him, Joanna behind me, and the rest of the group behind her, with Laik bringing up the rear. I keep waiting for the moment that someone falls into the rushing water below. Since it's spring, the river is moving faster than it does other times of the year. I'm not sure that I'd survive a fall, lycan strength or not. Swimming was Willow's talent, not mine.

Sweat beads along my hairline, and I hold my breath for what feels like ages. I take a wrong step, and my left foot slides out from under me. Pain courses up my leg as it scrapes across the metal and concrete. I hold in a yelp and scramble to hang on, squeezing my eyes tight, but my fingers slip from the rail, and I fall.

CHAPTER 17

Joanna is quick. She grabs hold of my arm and yanks me up. I grip the rail for a moment, tears welling in my eyes, as I gasp to catch my breath. I reach down and pat my leg. There's blood, but the cut is shallow, and though it stings, it won't affect my ability to walk. If what I've learned about lycans is true, it'll heal fast.

I'm okay… Sure, I almost died, but what's new?

My mind may make jokes, but my heart pounds and my stomach churns. I give Joanna a nod, and we continue on. Eventually, we make it to the other side, and the moment my feet are on solid ground, I want to lie down and kiss it. The thought of having to leave the city the same way makes me want to throw up. I hope we'll have a boat or that we'll get to leave another way, because I don't ever want to cross that bridge again. I hadn't realized that I was scared of heights, but now I know.

This part of the city is as equally run down as the

bridge, but I understand why we came this way. We're near the nice area where Ryne lives.

And now Elle too.

Grady keeps to the back alleyways as we maneuver through the sleeping city. We cross behind a mating house at one point, and the voices of men and women laughing scatter into the night. I swallow hard, wishing I could run in there and free those women. It reminds me why I'm even here and doing this. It would be selfish to hide away when I could help people break free from this awful system.

The other two groups splinter off, and ours keeps going. I start to feel disoriented because we're in the rundown part of the city that was too far lost to the wars to bother restoring. But after a few blocks, we leave that behind and enter into the neighborhood where the betas live. Being here sends opposing emotions racing through me--fear and love, longing and hatred. I don't know the houses, but I'd recognize this neighborhood anywhere. When the back of Ryne's stately house comes into view, my heart tightens. I know he's not in there right now because Madame Delphine lured him away, but I still miss him. I miss him so much that I forget to breathe.

Then I remember that he married Elle, and apparently, he's not been kind to her. That knowledge is so at odds with the man I knew that it's hard to believe, but I must believe it because that man also hurt people--hurt me, his own mate.

How can I love and hate him so much at the same time? *Damn you, Ryne.* And damn me for feeling this way.

I stare up with trepidation. It's late, and the house is

completely dark. We scale the backyard fence, landing in the cover of mature trees. The climb was easy for me, way easier than it would've been when I was still human. I don't know what to do with that information, but I have to admit it felt amazing to scale that fence as if it was nothing.

The yard is cast in shadows, the swimming pool is a black mirror, and the trees are eerily still. It's so quiet I can hear my heart pounding. The house itself is grand and intimidating, and I can't help but question how Grady is going to get inside. He sprints over to one of the flowerbeds near the back door, overturns a rock and picks something up, then returns to us, revealing a shiny silver key. It's the strangest thing, but I instinctively want to knock the key out of his hand. Him knowing about Ryne's spare key is proof they were close friends. And now he's going to use that to break into Ryne's home and kidnap his wife. Not kidnap--rescue--but Ryne and his pack won't see it that way. I can already imagine the awful things King Thorn will say to Ryne when news of this inevitably comes out.

I clench my hands into fists and will the urge away. I must think of Elle--she needs our help, even if it means exploiting Grady's knowledge of Ryne's home.

Grady gathers us together so that we can all hear his whisper. "Joanna and Poppy take the first floor, Laik and I will take the second, and Cici and Michael will take the third. Search every room. When you are finished, you come back outside and meet by that tree." He points to a large oak on the edge of the property. "With a little luck and a lot of stealth, we'll have Elle with us."

The second floor is where the bedrooms are, and I

expect that's where they will find Elle, so it makes sense that Grady would want to do that himself. I'm grateful that he trusts me with Joanna. Quite frankly, I'm a little surprised he wanted Laik with him, but maybe he's just giving Joanna and me time together. He's a good man, and I'm glad he and Joanna have each other. And knowing Grady, he also wants to keep an eye on the lycan alpha.

We sneak into the house and all go our separate ways. If my heart was pounding before, it's thrashing now. Sweat forms on my brow, and my stomach is so tight I could be sick. I'm terrified, and I need to get it together. What am I so afraid of anyway? Seeing Ryne? I won't see him since he's not here. Getting caught? That's it. If they catch me, they'll kill me without question.

I pause in the living room and just stare at the couch for a moment, my throat clogging up a bit. That's where I tended to Ryne's wounds. The memories flood me, and I'm brought right back to heartache. At least it drowns out the fear. Joanna tugs on my arm, and I shake the memories away. I need to focus.

We quickly move through the first floor, but there is no one here. I expected a guard of some sort, but Madame Delphine was right. There's nobody. Joanna waves me on, and we slip back outside and wait by the tree.

"Was it hard being back in the house?" Joanna asks, her voice soft.

I nod but don't elaborate. Confessing the details about Ryne and myself will just make things harder. I'm doing my best to put that all behind me.

We wait in silence, and soon the others are back. "No sign of Elle?" Grady asks.

We all shake our heads. Grady jams a hand through his hair. "We have to get her out of this mess. I have no idea where else she would be."

"We could just ask Ryne," Michael says with a smirk.

"What's that supposed to mean?" I ask. My voice sounds weird coming out, like it belongs to someone else.

"He's asleep upstairs in the library."

Laik's eyes sparkle. "Excellent. Let's kill him."

Something squeezes in my chest. As much as I'm upset that he betrayed me, he did let me go when he should've killed me. And he's my fated mate, so even though we'll never be together, the assurance that he's alive is a comfort to me. I can't explain why.

Grady nods. "It's the perfect opportunity."

My heart sinks even more. If Grady is on board, then it's practically a done deal. Even though they were friends, I understand why Grady would want to do it--Ryne nearly killed him and took his arm. He'll never be whole again, and that's all Ryne's fault. As much as Ryne betrayed me, he betrayed his friend even more.

I think fast, trying to find a good argument for why we shouldn't kill him.

"No. We can't do it," I say.

Grady glares at me. "Why not?" Though he knows exactly why I'm arguing with him. At least he hasn't said anything.

"Because..." My mind scrambles for an explanation. "We all know that even though Ryne is Carolina Pack's alpha, he's not the worst possible person for the job. If he dies, Anders becomes the alpha, and he's even worse."

"She has a point." Joanna looks to the others who don't

know Anders from Ryne. "Anders is a vile man. He'll make the mating houses a worse hell than they already are. He's talked openly of wanting to bring more girls in, he may even start raiding the villages."

They consider this, but I can tell they're not convinced.

"Look, what if we just kidnap him?" I offer. "Bring him back to the lycan camp for interrogation and send the wolf pack into a frenzy. They might even think he's gone on a trip before they realize we took him, and by then we'll be long gone."

"Same thing, hon," Joanna frowns. "Anders will become the alpha."

I shake my head. "No, don't you remember this from our lessons? As long as Ryne's alive, the pack will instinctively know it. It will cause chaos here because they won't be able to replace him with Anders. They can't, at least not permanently until the pack bond breaks."

"That's brilliant." Cici chuckles low. "And maybe we can send another group in to kill Anders. Hell, I'll volunteer."

"So will I," Michael adds.

I nod eagerly. "And while Ryne's being interrogated, we can find out what they did with Elle. She should be here. We can come back for her once we know where they're really keeping her."

Grady's eyes are hard, but I can tell he's considering it.

Laik releases a low growl. "If we take the alpha, he's coming back to my camp, and I can't guarantee I won't end up killing him there if he doesn't cooperate."

I hate to think of what Laik will do to Ryne, but this plan gives me some time. I can find a way to get him out of Laik's clutches before they kill him. Plus, I have some questions of my own that I want to ask. He has some serious explaining to do about why he still went through with his marriage to Elle.

We all go silent for a long minute. Grady and Joanna exchange a knowing look and then turn to me. "What do you think? Can you lure him out?" Joanna asks gently.

Grady explains to the others, "Ryne has a soft spot for Poppy."

"Now why would he have a soft spot for Poppy?" Laik asks gruffly, his hooded eyes zeroed in on me.

I swallow hard because this is the last thing I want to explain to Laik of all people. "He took a liking to me during the claiming and often sought my company. I wasn't an idiot, so I encouraged it. It's the reason he sent Knox with me after I was bit, and why I wasn't immediately executed. He cares for me."

Something unreadable passes over Laik's face. "And do you care for him?"

If I lie, he'll see right through it. "I do."

"Then you will stay here while the rest of us go inside."

"No." Joanna shakes her head. "Ryne will have weapons near him, and he can shift at any moment, unlike you. He'll fight. He knows his house better than anyone else. Getting him down three flights of stairs will be impossible. If Poppy can lure him out here, we can be waiting with everything we need to knock him out and kidnap him."

I wouldn't have thought of that, but she's right.

"She could just as easily warn him, and he'll get away," Laik challenges.

"He betrayed me." I stand tall, unwavering in this. "I

have no love for him anymore. I'll get him out here, and you can do whatever you need to subdue him."

Lies. All lies.

Before Laik can protest anymore, I'm running across the yard, not bothering to look back. They can't call out to stop me because that would give them away. My thoughts whirl as I run. What if Ryne hates me? I've betrayed him as much as he betrayed me. For all I know, he'll kill me the second he sees me. Maybe this wasn't a good idea after all. But I couldn't let them kill him, no matter how much he hurt me. Though, Ryne won't see it that way. I could just warn him, but Laik would take revenge out on Knox and Charlotte, and they've been through enough.

I was never clumsy before, but it's amazing how my limbs move much easier now that I'm a lycan. It's effortless to climb up the stairs and not make a sound, to slip through the halls and into the library. I close the door behind me with a soft click, and my eyes adjust to the room instantly. One of the curtains is open, and soft blue light streams in from the large waning moon, casting shadows along the floor-to-ceiling bookshelves. Ryne is on the couch, and I step forward, needing to go to him. Nerves dance in my belly, and I can't tell if they are good or bad ones.

I approach, drinking in his long black curls and sharp, smooth cheekbones. His lips are soft, and his eyelids flutter and pop open. He blinks several times. "Poppy? Am I dreaming?"

CHAPTER 18

I shake my head, at a loss for words. Now that I'm here in front of him, every fiber of my being longs to go to him and never leave his arms. I clench my fists at my sides, angry at myself for being so weak. He's not mine anymore. He's Elle's and I need to ask him where she is.

He's out of his chair in one fluid movement. His large hands palm my cheeks, and he stares into my eyes. "I've missed you so much."

Without warning, his lips are on mine, moving furiously, and all thought and space disappears. It's just me and him. My arms clutch his neck, and his hands slip down to my side, pulling me taut against his warm body. He teases my lip with his tongue, and I let him in, hungry for more of this man. I want nothing more than for this moment to never end. All the emotions of the last month spill out into this kiss like ink seeping onto paper, messy and beautiful and permanent. It's not fair. We should've been together. It should've been us. But now he belongs to another, and I've become his worst enemy.

Something shifts between us, a softness I'm not expecting. All at once, he goes limp in my arms, his towering frame falling forward onto me. We collapse to the ground, his weight too much for me. I hit my head on the hardwood, and stars flash before my eyes. He's on top of me, his dead weight heavy, and the breath whooshes from my lungs. I'm trapped beneath his unconscious body.

I have no idea what just happened.

"Ryne?" I whisper and push against him, but it's like pushing against a brick wall. He's not moving. "Ryne?" I say louder, panic in my voice. His heady smell envelops me, rich with sleep, but there's no way this is sleep. People don't just fall asleep like that. My oxygen grows thin as I try to wiggle out from under him, but I can't move either. Panic starts to set in like claws dragging across my skin. I won't last long. He's too big.

I keep pushing. I should be stronger than this. The moon is almost full, and I'm not the girl I once was. For weeks--months--I've longed to be next to him, to feel his limbs tangled with mine, but this is torture. I finally get my wish, and he's going to suffocate me.

"Ryne!" I scream this time and thrash against him. He groans slightly and shifts his weight, but not in the direction I need. He's even more on top of me now, and there's no breath left to scream again. Stars are still dancing around my vision, growing dim as a black tunnel closes in, turning the ceiling into darkness.

And then Ryne is gone.

I gasp, sucking in air and coughing. My vision returns, and I sit up. The others surround us on all sides.

"What happened?" Joanna asks.

Laik kicks at Ryne's side, laughing. "Did you go ahead and kill him?"

"No." I swallow, and my throat burns. "He kissed me and then passed out."

They all give me a strange look.

"We need to get out of here. We've already taken too much time." Laik crouches down next to Ryne and begins tying up his arms and legs.

"Why can't you guys just shift when you're tied up?" I ask Grady. But he's distracted by something Joanna is whispering to him.

The way I figure it, the wolves should be able to shift out of whatever binding they're in. Keeping Ryne as our prisoner isn't going to be easy. It's not like we have other shifters with us to guard him, and I've seen what the man is capable of.

If they don't take him as a prisoner, they really will kill him. I have zero doubt it's something Laik has been trying to do for years, and I've delivered Ryne right to him.

"We're sensitive to silver, but they're sensitive to wolfsbane," Laik says as he finishes tying Ryne's limbs. "Not that they would've told you that."

"What's wolfsbane?"

He snorts. "It's a plant. It's woven into the fibers of this rope."

I eye the rope with a frown. I didn't know he'd brought it along. This action may be small to everyone else, but it's big to me, lending another reason to distrust Laik. The man is more calculating than he lets on. The mission was to free Elle--nothing that would've required wolfsbane threaded rope. I know better than to question Laik about it, but I tuck the information away for later, reminding myself to keep a close eye on things once we're back at camp.

We all gather around to carry Ryne from the house. It takes everyone helping because Ryne is so big, and I grimace when some people are less than gentle with his body. I want to talk about this—I'm practically overflowing with the need, but we have to stay silent, and I'm distracted by Ryne's head. I'm the one who's holding it. His cheeks are warm, and his long hair is silky. I want to kiss him again, which is ridiculous. He's not my lover. He's not even my friend. We're on opposite sides of a war, and there's no defending his side anymore. He's in the wrong, and as much as I love him, I have to accept that he's the bad guy. Even if Thorn is the worst of them, even if Ryne never slept with the mating house girls, even if he dreamed of ways to make changes, even if his kiss makes me feel the most like myself, the fact remains that he's the alpha of this pack. He's made his choices.

And we're done.

Laik leads us away from the beta houses and around the deserted parts of the city until we reach the riverbank. We're so quiet as we go, so slow and methodical in our movements among the shadows. Twice people roam by, but they don't notice us. I'm grateful they're not in wolf form because I think they probably would've sensed us then.

I gaze out at the river and release a shuddering breath.

"What's the plan here?" My heart has started to race--I have a bad feeling about this.

"I hope you can all swim," Laik says nonchalantly. "And if you can't, drop him. Their alpha can drown for all I care."

I'm not a good swimmer, but it's not me I'm worried about.

"No--" My voice breaks, and I'm given the death stare by everyone here. Even Joanna doesn't care if Ryne dies. "He's not valuable to us dead, remember? Anders . . ." My voice speeds up. "Anders is so much worse than Ryne and you know it. We already agreed!" I look down at Ryne, where we've set him on the dirt. How is he still unconscious?

"Wait. Will the pack be able to track him to the lycan camp?" Cici asks skeptically.

Grady answers, but I can tell he hates giving away this kind of information. He may not be a part of the pack anymore, but his roots still run deep. "We know if our alpha is dead or alive, not where he is."

"Are you sure?" Cici frowns. "I'm not lycan, so I'm not going back to the lycan camp, but I don't want to lead wolves there either."

"He's not my alpha anymore--"

"Enough," Laik cuts in. "The camp is under my protection." There's a double meaning behind his words, but I'm not sure what it is. It's almost as if he doesn't want to have this conversation in front of Grady, which is strange, but considering Grady is a wolf shifter, maybe not. "The alpha lives. For now. So let's keep his head above water, huh?" A sour grin mars his face.

A few of the others laugh, but I can't. The water is high,

and the currents are dangerous. Swimming in this river could mean death, but there's no other way to get Ryne out of the city quickly. The sun will be up soon, and it's only a matter of time until we're being tracked by the wolves.

This stupid plan was all mine, but I'm pretty sure I made a mistake.

Laik must sense my trepidation. "Don't worry, little lycan, we make great swimmers. You'll see once you're in the water. And as for Ryne, the water and the wolfsbane will help mask his scent." He peers back out at the city, his jaw clenching and unclenching. "Don't forget we're moving camp again soon. I know how to stay one step ahead of these dogs." He turns back to offer Grady a cocky grin. "No offense."

Grady sighs but doesn't reply.

I hope Laik is right, but there's nothing more to say, and there's little time left. So against my better judgment, I follow them into the river and try to stay alive.

CHAPTER 19

The river is colder than I expected. Maybe because my blood runs hotter than it did when I was a human. I don't like it one bit, but I manage to keep my head above water and Ryne's head resting on my shoulder. Laik is right that I'm a much better swimmer now that I've become a lycan, and for the first time since my renewal, I'm glad for it.

We're all soaked to the bone when we reach the other shore, but nobody is lost to the currents, and I thank my lucky stars for that. Cici and Michael splinter off to report back to the Resistance members who will be waiting for us. They'll explain that we didn't find Elle, but we hope to find answers about her once our new prisoner wakes up.

Laik refuses to go anywhere but back to his camp with Ryne in tow. Grady and Joanna insist on coming back with us even though I'm sure Grady will hate being among the lycan. Laik doesn't fight him on it, which surprises everyone.

Ryne is heavier now that we've got river water weighing us down and Cici and Michael are gone, but we manage to get to the truck. I nearly cry out in relief when we do.

By the time we drop off the truck and shuffle back into camp hours later, I'm shivering madly and ice-cold despite the May air being hot and humid. It's going to be a ferocious summer out here in the wilds, but right now I'd give just about anything for some of that warmth.

I change quickly and meet Grady, Joanna, Knox, and Charlotte outside my tent. Knowing Ryne is not far makes me itch to be near him, but I know that's not possible. I'm not even sure why I want to see him, and I'm glad my friends are here to distract me.

"Are you guys staying long?" I ask her, hopeful. If Joanna stays, I'll have my best friend back.

"Don't know yet, but I want to be here when Ryne wakes up and realizes he's been betrayed by his girl," Grady answers, giving me a bitter smirk. It's not that he wants to hurt me, but he wants to see Ryne suffer, and my heart tightens at that.

They were best friends.

"Ryne's here?" Knox asks, his face going pale. I'm still not exactly sure where Knox's loyalties lie when it comes to Ryne.

"Yeah. Poppy totally kissed him, and he passed out. Kidnapping him was easy," Joanna says with a cheeky grin. The smile is so *her* that I want to burst into tears and tackle her in a hug. I didn't realize how lonely I was.

"Why did he pass out?" Charlotte's eyebrows knit together.

"Because of Poppy's saliva," Callum announces from behind me.

I spin and find him and Laik. Callum eyes Grady's stump. I know he's just doing it because of his medical background, but Grady doesn't know that, and he gives him a hostile glare. Callum drops his eyes.

"What do you mean by my saliva?" I ask.

Callum looks at us for a long moment, as if deciding if he can trust us with this information. "It's a theory I've had for a while. We know that wolf shifters can be poisoned by our bites, but I don't think our fangs are the only thing that's venomous. I was pretty sure our saliva is dangerous for them too. Well, I was right, and you've just confirmed it."

My mouth pops open. "I poisoned him?" Of all the times lycan have tried to bite and kill him, who would've thought a kiss would've done it?

"He's alive and seems okay, so our saliva must not be as lethal as our actual bite. Either that or it's not as potent as it would've been during a full moon. He just woke up, and he's spitting mad."

I swallow. I almost killed Ryne, and I didn't even mean to. Does this mean I can never kiss him again? Of course, I can't. Our situation was already impossible to begin with, but now it feels like we're cursed. I want to cry, to scream, to break something, but I can't show that kind of emotion in front of these people, so I force myself to stay calm.

"We need you to go in there and kiss him again. But only a small one. We want him subdued, not knocked out," Laik says.

I cross my arms. "He's not going to go for that. At this point, he'll know I betrayed him."

"Actually, he won't. We're going to dump you in there all tied up, but loosely so you can get out of them easily. Then you kiss him, and we'll come in and interrogate him. You can help."

"You want my help?" I squeak. I eye Laik with skepticism. From day one we haven't seen eye to eye, but now that I'm useful to him, he suddenly needs me? *I don't think so, buddy.*

"Yeah. He'll probably talk to you before he'll talk to one of us. If he cares for you as much as you think he does, then it should be easy."

"Not if he thinks I betrayed him," I try again.

Laik shrugs. "We'll see. The sooner we get answers from him, the sooner we can kill the bastard."

I clear my throat. "If I help you, what's in it for me?"

Laik scoffs. "How about I don't kill you?"

I raise an eyebrow and nod because he does have a point. As much as I hate it, he's the one in power here. Not me. Hopefully I can do something to change that before everyone I care about ends up dead. Joanna gives me a funny look--she's probably following my train of thought and knows I'll risk my life for Ryne. I follow Laik, and Joanna slips her arm through mine.

"What's your plan?" she whispers.

"What do you mean?" I feign innocence.

"Oh, come on, I know how the bond works. There is no way in Hades you're going to let Ryne die, even if that's what everyone else wants. So what's your plan?"

"I don't have one. Not yet anyway." It feels good

confiding in her even though I'm still confused. Everything moved so fast. I will find a way to get Ryne out of there before he dies. Even though he betrayed me and married Elle, I still love him.

We stop outside Laik's tent, and he glances at Joanna. "What are you still doing here?"

"Poppy's my best friend. I'm here to support her."

Laik rolls his eyes. "Poppy doesn't need any help. Go back to your dog, and Callum will get you guys set up in a tent. This will take a couple of days. Cici and Michael will let the Resistance know that we need Anders dead. Once it's confirmed that the alpha's second in command is no longer in the picture, we can kill Ryne." He gives Joanna an annoyed look. "We don't need you for that, little girl."

Joanna is stiff, and I can tell she's got fire on her tongue, just waiting to spit it out at Laik.

"It's okay. You can go," I say. "You can't come into the tent with me anyway."

Joanna gives me a strained smile and rushes back to Grady. Laik goes into his tent and comes back out with rope and a gag. I let him tie me up, and like he said, I'm bound loose enough that I can get out but tight enough to look real.

Then he hoists me over his shoulder a little too roughly. We walk about thirty feet, and he opens the tent flap. I catch a quick glance at Ryne before Laik dumps me on the ground. My head hits the packed earth, and I see stars.

As soon as Laik is gone, I sit up. Ryne has a bag over his head, and he's straining against his bonds. Muffled sounds come from under the bag. I'm guessing they have him gagged as well.

I easily slip out of the ropes tying my hands together and then rip off my gag. I have no idea why he even bothered to tie me up when Ryne can't see me. Probably his idea of a sick joke.

"It's me," I say. "I'm tied up, but I managed to get my hands out. Let me get my feet undone, and then I'll help you. We'll need to move fast."

He stills, but I have no idea what he's thinking. It takes me a little longer to untie my feet because Laik tied those ropes tighter, but within moments I have them undone as well. I think about untying Ryne and trying to run away with him now, but we'll never make it. Laik and several others stand right outside the tent door at the moment. I'll have to wait until people are sleeping, and we can slip away unnoticed. Maybe I'll get him out and stay back. Saving his life doesn't mean I have to bring myself to be around him anymore.

I pull the hood off his head, and Ryne blinks at me, his hair a mess. I get to work on the knot on the back of his gag, but it's tied tightly. My fingers slip and slide but eventually find purchase, and I'm able to undo it. I tear it off.

"Poppy, what's going on?" he asks, a razored-edge to his tone.

"I don't know, but we're going to get out of here. I've missed you so much." My voice cracks. Can he sense the torture I feel inside? I need to be strong right now. Ryne might not realize after that first kiss that I betrayed him, but he will after this one. Before I can even think about what I'm doing, I lick my lips and press them against his. It's a quick kiss because I can't risk a bigger one, and I pull away.

His taut body immediately goes limp, but he's still conscious. His sorrowful eyes meet mine. "Poppy, what did you do?"

Laik enters then, giving a slow clap. "Well done, Poppy. We couldn't have subdued him without you."

He crouches in front of Ryne. "Now, let's see what information you can give us."

A couple of other men come in. I don't remember their names because I've never spoken to them, but they are two of Laik's go-to guards. I don't know what they are going to do to Ryne, and I don't want to watch them.

One grabs my hands, and the other grabs my feet. They tie me up again, but tighter this time, and put a gag on me. I'm so startled that I don't process what's happening fast enough to fight them off.

"Now, we aren't sure what your connection to Poppy is, but based on how you reacted to her, we expect you would do anything to help her. Otherwise, why would you send your man with her out into the woods instead of just killing her? You've shown before that you're willing to kill any and all lycan," Laik says.

He just looks at them through a dazed glaze. I wonder if he can even hear them. I don't know how badly my saliva affected him.

"Tell us where Elle is."

His gaze sharpens, and I know he heard the question. Instead of answering, he spits in Laik's face.

Laik wipes the spit off and stands. "You know, if I were to return that favor, you'd be unconscious again. Lucky for you, I want you conscious."

He turns to the men standing by me. "Break her finger."

CHAPTER 20

Panic blooms in my chest as one of the men slams his boot down on my left pinky and twists. For a moment, I feel nothing but shock. No pain, no comprehension of what happened. I glance down. My pinky is bleeding and turned in the wrong direction. Then all at once, pain sears through my hand and radiates up my arm. I cry out, and Ryne yells, "No!"

Laik chuckles. "I knew you'd come around."

I try to keep from whimpering. I don't want Laik to have any more ammo to use on Ryne. As much as I want to hate Ryne, right now, I hate Laik more. This is how he wanted me to help him? This is like the sick game that he played with me and Knox. And here I am, the stupid girl who should've stopped trusting men like him long ago.

The pain is horrible, but not as bad as I expect it to be. At the back of my mind, I know I'm not human anymore. I'll heal quickly, but I'll have to get Callum to set it for me first. I don't think I can do it myself. Soon this agony will be in the past, but right now I'd love nothing more than to claw Laik's eyes out.

Ryne hesitates for a moment, searching my face before looking up at Laik with disdain. "I don't know where Elle is. After she married my father, I helped her escape, but I don't know where she went, and my father made me swear to keep her disappearance a secret."

I let out an audible gasp. He didn't marry Elle. *His father did.* I want to ask him what happened and tell him I'm sorry and beg for his forgiveness. But I can't because of the gag.

Laik studies him and then me. Tears flow from my eyes, but I can't say anything. Maybe they'll all think it's because of the pain, but the pain is only part of why I'm crying.

"Where's the king alpha?" Laik sneers, bending down to get in Ryne's face.

Ryne only shrugs. "When he's in my city, he usually stays at my house, but tonight he was called away. He's been on the hunt for Elle but not having much luck, and it's been getting to him, leading him out of the city more often than not." His eyes narrow at that. "Careful, lycan, Thorn may venture to your little camp here."

Laik grins. "I'm not worried about us. If he does somehow show up here, that will give us the opportunity to kill him."

Ryne is unchanged, but I can see his brain processing everything: these men, this cramped canvas tent, the wolfsbane bindings at his hands and feet. Everything. "Well, he usually takes my man Anders to help search for her, so you'd be fighting off two wolves."

"Why wouldn't he take you? You're his son, an alpha, a *prince*."

"Because he trusts Anders with the secret of his missing bride, and he doesn't entirely trust me after Poppy . . ." Ryne trails off, not finishing the statement, and my heart pounds.

"After Poppy what?" Laik asks.

"After she sabotaged my wedding with Elle." It's sort of true. It's better than him saying that I'm his fated. But I suppose if this keeps going on like this, Laik is bound to figure it out. I still don't know what he'll do with that information, but I'm certain it won't be good.

"Now why would she do that?" From what I've told Laik, I was encouraging Ryne's advances to get by.

"Because she's in love with me. Has been since she arrived in my city, but I always told her we could never be together. Don't mistake me. Poppy is a beautiful girl, and I dated her, but I never intended to marry her. She knew I was engaged to Elle. She didn't listen though."

He gives me a scathing look, and I wonder if anything in his expression is true. These lies are meant to help me--I know that--and yet they still twist me up inside.

"But you do care for her." Laik stands and comes to my side. "If you didn't, seeing her in pain wouldn't cause you to open your mouth."

Ryne scowls through inky strands of hair that have fallen across his face. "I don't like seeing any woman in pain. If you'd brought another in here and done the same thing, I still would have talked."

"I doubt that's true." He kicks my side. "You like this one."

Ryne sighs. "What I'm telling you isn't a secret that I need to keep from you anyway, so can we just get on with this."

Laik scratches his chin, and I know he's trying to figure out if Ryne is lying or not. "You really don't like seeing *any* woman in pain? That's the biggest lie you've told me all day, *alpha dog*." He says alpha like it's a curse word, and I know he's referring to the way the shifters treat human women.

"I'm not lying." Ryne looks at me, his eyes narrowed. "I hate the way the harvest and mating houses work. I've been trying to make changes for years, but I'm not the one in charge of these things. My job is to enforce the rules and keep order in my city and nothing more."

"Spare us the bullshit." Laik moves to tower over him, and the two lock in a glare.

"I'm serious," Ryne seethes between gritted teeth. "I was getting close to a solution, and then you kidnapped me. Now who's going to help those women? You?" He cackles. "You can't take on my father, and if you think you can, you're an idiot."

Laik kicks him then, hard and dead-center. Ryne coughs but nothing more. Everything goes quiet for what feels like ages. In that pause, my finger starts to throb again. I'm not as strong as I thought I was, but I need to be. I don't want to draw attention to myself.

Finally, Laik nods to the men guarding me. "Take Poppy to the medic's tent. We're done for today." He crouches in front of Ryne. "I have men in your city. If I find out you're lying, then I will kill Poppy right in front of you. Do you want to change your story? This is your last chance to come clean."

Ryne shakes his head, and I'm roughly brought to my feet. They drag me out of there, and Ryne just stares after me. There's so much I want to tell him, but I can't. Not right now. But after I'm healed, I'll come back here and tell him how sorry I am and that I'll get him out of here and do anything else he needs. He says he had a plan to take down Thorn, that he's been wanting to change things for years, and deep down I know that's the honest truth. I was never able to reconcile the cruel alpha with the tender man I fell for, and now I know why. My heart was right all along--Ryne isn't bad.

I can't believe I doubted him.

Ten days pass--ten long, arduous, awful days--where they don't let me see him. Ten days where I'm put to work doing manual labor that leaves my muscles burning, my sleep deep, and my free time completely consumed. I never complain, hoping that it will get me in good graces with Laik. I ask Laik to see Ryne every single day, and he always says no. Always.

It's after another one of these dead-end conversations that I find myself stalking through the woods, muttering nasty things about Laik under my breath and kicking trees.

"What did them trees ever do to you, huh?" Wanda's scratchy voice makes me jump, and I whip around to find her. She's watching me with amused eyes and a yellow smile.

I glare. "Has your boyfriend always been such an ass?"

Her smile falls. "If it weren't for Laik's generosity, you'd be long dead. I'd have killed you and your little alpha-boy and been done with the lot of you ages ago. But for some reason, Laik thinks you'll be more valuable to us alive." She shrugs her bony shoulders. "Lucky for you, I trust Laik."

"I've already proven myself to you people," I practically shout. "What more could you possibly want from me?"

She stalks in close, her sour-sweet scent wrapping me up. "You already know. Don't pretend you don't."

I still, realizing she's right. Swear loyalty and take Laik as my alpha. It's not something I ever plan on doing, but I have the sinking suspicion that's what he's waiting for. Eventually, he's going to grow tired of waiting, and then what? Will he kill me? What about Joanna and Grady? Knox? Charlotte? The man has so many of my friends under his care right now.

And not from the goodness of his heart.

"You have nothing to say?" she chuckles and walks away. "That's what I thought. We're leaving, by the way. Laik told me to come find you."

I chase after her. "What? We're leaving?"

"Yeah, caught wind of wolves nearby. We need to retreat closer to panther territory."

So maybe now I'll finally get to see Ryne, and that excites me, but I'm also filled with dread at the prospect of wolf shifters nearby. It stands to reason they're out looking for their missing alpha. Quite frankly, I'm surprised we've gone as long as we have undetected. It doesn't really make sense. The wolves are hunters, and we're not that far from their city. How are any of the lycan still alive out here? We get one day a month to be powerful, and they can call upon their beasts at any time.

"How come they can't find us out here?" I ask, hoping I'll get lucky. "There are so many more of them than us."

"They're not great at following a lycan's scent." I'm surprised she answered so quickly but grateful all the same. "Especially near the full moon. Do you believe in God?"

She turns on me again, this time pinning me against a tree. I fold my arms over my chest and stand tall. I'm not scared of her, and I don't want her to think I am. "I don't know what I believe anymore," is all I say. My parents believed in God, and Mama taught us about that stuff, but I haven't thought of God very much lately. Her mention of him now catches me by surprise.

"Well, I do," she says. "I know we're here to stop the shifters, and that includes your precious Ryne. Wanna know how I know?"

I don't ask, but she answers anyway.

"Because our saliva is their poison. Because when we bite humans, we can easily make more of us. Because God made the moon, and we're beholden to that moon. And because those dogs can't follow our scent to save their own lives."

She kind of has a point, but does God really want us to kill each other? Because if God is real, and he made us, then he also made them too.

She must think this is hysterical because she walks away, laughing the entire way back to camp. Her words stick in my mind, and I examine them at all angles. I was Ryne's fated mate, and now I'm his enemy. But what was that story Mama always told us? The one with the lion befriending the lamb?

Perhaps there's a bigger purpose here--a reason for everything that's happened to me. Ryne and I are still fated, that much I can sense to my core. Turning into a lycan didn't take my feelings away, and if anything, they've only grown stronger. Someone has to save the humans. Maybe Ryne and I are meant to do that together.

CHAPTER 21

The camp is in complete disarray. People are taking down tents, loading food into carts, and stuffing their backpacks. They scurry about, an air of practiced panic at their heels. We've moved several times since I've been with them, but the energy is so different now that there's a known threat in the area. The only tent still up is Ryne's, and I take a step closer to it. How is he doing? Probably not well. I asked Callum last night at dinner if he was at least getting food. Callum was vague but assured me Ryne was okay.

I find Laik talking with Grady and Joanna. Everyone shuts up when I approach, and I grow uneasy. "What do you need me to do?" I ask.

"Nothing. I thought you were gathering wood in the forest." Laik's voice is gruff.

"I was, but do you really want me to carry wood to a new camp?" I shrug. "Anyway, Wanda came and told me you needed me."

Laik runs a hand along his face. "Of course she did. That woman never listens to me."

Wanda approaches with a wicked knife in her hands. "Can I do the honors?" She shakes the blade in my face.

"What's she talking about?" I ask, now concerned.

"We can't haul Ryne with us," Laik says.

My stomach tightens. "You can't kill him!"

Laik rubs his eyes. "See, Wanda, this is why you should've left her in the woods."

I glance over at Joanna. "You guys were going to let him die?"

Grady gives me a frown. "Ryne isn't being the most cooperative prisoner, and you knew he was going to die here eventually."

"You can't mean that." I scramble for something else to say. "Besides, you guys said you wanted Anders dead first."

"Unfortunately, the Resistance didn't agree with us on that one," Laik snaps. "Fools, all of them if you ask me, but we can't execute Anders without their help. Not yet, anyway."

I hate the way he speaks about the Resistance like they're a tool for him to use, not like he's part of them, like we're all in this together. "Okay, but Anders being alive is exactly why we kept Ryne alive too. The Resistance not seeing eye to eye with us is still not a good reason to kill Ryne."

Grady points to his stump of an arm. "This is his fault, and don't forget that he would've done worse if I hadn't gotten out of there. Isn't that a good enough reason for you, Poppy?"

Joanna scowls at him but doesn't say anything to defend me either. I can't believe she's okay with this.

"But . . . but . . . he said he was working against his father. He helped Elle escape, we know that now. Why do you want to kill him?" This question is mainly for Grady, because even after everything that's happened, I suspect he must still care for his ex-best friend and alpha. There's got to be something left.

"He's a wolf, isn't he?" Joanna finally speaks up. "That makes him our enemy. I'm sorry, Poppy, but it does."

I point to Grady. "Um, excuse me, but he's a wolf too!"

"You know what I mean. Listen, we heard this morning that Anders has been doing a lot of awful things in the city." She gives me a pointed look and even more weight is added to my shoulders. "Who cares if Anders is a stand-in alpha when he now has the power to do whatever the hell he wants. Our plan backfired, so keeping Ryne alive is pointless." Tears spring to my eyes and her voice softens. "I'm sorry, but if we kill Ryne now, the shifters will be able to feel that they've lost their alpha through the pack bond, and then all hell will break loose in wolf city while they fight each other for his title."

"And one of the other wolves might stop Anders," Grady adds.

I have to admit, their logic makes sense, and I'm seconds away from falling to my knees and begging.

Laik smiles broadly. "The chaos we're about to create will give us the perfect opportunity to take them down."

"Ryne's already been kidnapped and imprisoned and who knows what else!" I throw my hands in the air. "Isn't that enough?"

"No," Grady snaps. "As long as he's alive, the pack is going to remain united. We need to do this now. Hell, we should've done it already."

"While we are at our weakest? Is that really what you want?" I turn to Laik because surely he needs to think about the safety of his people too. "If you kill Ryne, you'll have to answer to his father during a new moon." I point to the blue sky. "Have you forgotten that your precious moon will be weak tonight?"

"We can't let him go, and we can't take him with us," Laik barks. "The best option is to kill him."

"Please, don't." My voice cracks, and I dig my boot into the ground. A bead of sweat trickles down the back of my neck. "Too many people have died already."

Wanda slithers around the other side of me. "See, told you she was a snake. She's on their side, not ours."

"Just because she's sticking up for Ryne doesn't mean she's on their side," Joanna says, but Grady stiffens beside her.

Suddenly, hands grab me from behind. Two of Laik's bodyguards have a vise-like grip on my arms, their rough fingers digging into my skin.

"Come on, Grady, let's take care of him," Laik says, leaving me behind.

"No! You can't kill him!" I'm screaming and flailing, but I don't care. I need to save him. The need is as strong as my need to breathe--to live. I can't bear a world without Ryne in it.

"Joanna," I plead, but she just turns away from me. The brutes drag me away from the tent, but I can't let him die. I go limp in the hopes that they loosen their grip, but they hold on even tighter. I exhale in short little bursts, and my stomach twists. I can't lose another person that I love. I just can't.

A flash of silver shoots by us. "Wolf," someone screams, and the men holding me falter. Time seems to slow and then speed as they drop me and run after her. I do the same.

I'd know that silver wolf anywhere.

It's Elle.

She leaps onto Laik's back, and he goes down. Grady glances around, and Elle snarls at him. I reach them quickly and debate whether I should stop or head straight for Ryne.

If I leave her there, they might try to kill her.

Already, the whole place is descending on her. She's one of the strongest wolves I know, and the lycan are at our weakest with it being a new moon soon, but that doesn't mean she won't end up dead. I'll lose Ryne and Elle all in the same afternoon.

I rush forward, putting my hand on her back. "You have to change back, or they're going to kill you," I yell, knowing she can hear me, but so can the others. If I was doing a good job at hiding my alliances before, I've definitely ruined that now.

She glances at me like I'm crazy but then leaps off of Laik and shifts back into a human. She stands there, completely naked, her face livid.

"Callum," I yell. "Get her something to cover up with."

He finds a cart and grabs a blanket off of it. I hand it to Elle, who still hasn't said anything. She's lost weight since I last saw her, but her eyes have added a depth of angry bitterness that can only speak of hard times. ~~What has she been through?~~

"You can't kill Ryne," she grits out as she wraps the blanket around her torso.

Laik scrambles up. "Who are you?"

"I'm Elle. Ryne saved my life, and I know you've been looking for me. I've been following you for some time." Everyone goes quiet. "You can't kill him. He's the key to the resistance movement. I've been working on him for months, and he's finally agreed to help us." Her voice hardens. "You *cannot* kill him."

"You can't tell me what to do. Now, if you'll excuse me, I have a wolf to kill."

He turns back around and marches for the tent. Elle gives me a look, and I nod. We're not going to let this be Ryne's fate.

She shifts back into a wolf, and I'm right behind her. We both attack Laik, and soon Elle is on his chest, her jaws at his throat. He looks up at me, eyes wide. Others surround us, ready to defend their alpha, but he holds them off. Maybe he has too much pride, or maybe we all know Elle would kill him before they'd be able to stop her. It would take less than a second for his throat to be in her muzzle.

"You cannot kill him," I demand again. "Give us your word, and Elle will let you go. We didn't want to attack you, but Elle's right. He's too important to the Resistance. Let him join us, or let him go. Those are your only options."

Laik glares and then sighs heavily. "Fine, I won't kill him."

"Swear it on your honor as a lycan that you won't kill him or allow anyone else here to do it. He's under your protection now."

He growls under his breath and closes his eyes for a second. He's so enraged he's panting, but we've got him by the throat.

"I swear."

It's the best we're going to get, but from the frustrated looks on the other's faces, it's enough. Elle climbs off of him and shifts back into a human. This time, Callum hands her a shirt and pants.

"But I won't work with him either." Laik gets up and spits at our feet.

Elle rolls her eyes. "You're going to have to. I'll send word to Madame Delphine, and we'll go from there. The leader of the panther city should know as well."

"It's not fair that the panthers pretend to be neutral," I grumble. "They're clearly not." My face warms when I realize I said all this aloud.

Elle purses her lips. "They might be more open about their true feelings once they find out we have Ryne on our side. Good job getting him out."

"I don't think he'll see it that way."

She shrugs. "Let's go pay him a visit, shall we?"

"Wait." Laik holds up a hand. "This is my home and my pack. You can't come in here and take over."

"Actually, I can. Madame Delphine made me her second in command of the Resistance down here, so if you're working for the Resistance, you're working for me."

CHAPTER 22

The guards at the tent doors give us scathing looks but don't stop us from entering. We slide through the opening and find Ryne sitting in the back corner. I kneel down at his feet and begin fumbling with the wolfsbane ropes. I need to get them off him. Except for bathroom breaks, he's been trapped in here twenty-four-seven, and it's my fault.

He winces when I touch him, his eyes shiny and tired as they watch me through the curtain of his oily hair. "Not sure if I can trust you're actually helping me or not, but I heard what happened out there."

"You can." I bite my lip for a moment, thinking of what I could possibly say. "I didn't want to hurt you. I was trying to help."

He turns away and gazes up at Elle. "You were supposed to run away, and yet you can't be more than a day's walk from my city."

Elle shrugs. "You saved me. Now it's my turn."

I finish with the bindings and stand up.

"I could turn," he says, looking down on me. "I could turn and kill you right now, kill all your little friends too."

"These people aren't my friends," I shoot back. "Well, not all of them anyway. But we have bigger problems to worry about. Namely, your father."

"And let me guess, the lycan are magically going to help me now? How am I supposed to trust them?"

"They're with the Resistance," Elle points out. "And you don't have to trust them, but you can trust me."

"Well, that's one person," he snaps, and I deflate. He's mad at me, and I don't blame him, but it's not like he's entirely innocent here. He's the alpha in charge of the pack that killed my sister and enslaved so many. He's got blood on his hands, far more than I do. Still, I don't want him to hate me. I want to go back to what it felt like when he loved me. I want his kisses and his warmth and the promise of things to come.

"So what now?" he asks Elle.

"We move." Laik steps through the tent opening, his nostrils flaring. "We have two more weeks until the next full moon, and we're vulnerable here. Since Elle's demanding we keep you with us instead of killing you, you've become a liability."

"I didn't ask to be kidnapped." Ryne shakes his head. "I had a plan and knew what I was doing and--"

"I don't care." Laik cuts him off. "You're with us now, and I said we're moving out."

I want to say something more, or at the very least get a moment alone with Ryne to discuss everything that's happened, but he brushes past me like I'm nothing, and I'm the last to leave the tent.

Packing up is tense, but at least it's busy. There's no more time to fight. Everyone's got a job to do. I work alongside Callum and Charlotte. Elle and Ryne are on the other side of camp.

Once we start walking deeper into the woods, and the afternoon sun starts to fade, the tenseness among our ragtag group grows palpable. Everyone hates Elle, especially Laik. Everyone hates Ryne, especially Grady. And I'm pretty sure they all hate me. But at least we're alive.

We approach the camouflaged trucks, and Laik instructs half of the group to go to the panther city. "It'll be safer for you there. I'll send for you before the next full moon."

"What about him?" Someone points to Ryne. "Shouldn't he be sent away?"

"I can't go there." Ryne is quick to argue. "I'm forbidden. There's a treaty, and if I go there . . ." His voice falls away, and Elle shifts uncomfortably.

If he goes there, then that could be bad for his pack, which would actually be good for the Resistance, wouldn't it?

But nobody says anything more, and a few minutes later, our numbers are smaller than ever. There's Wanda, Laik, and four of his most trusted guards—three men and one woman. Callum also stays, and so do Charlotte and Knox. And then there's Elle, Ryne, and myself. Joanna and Grady stay with us as well, but I don't know why. Even though Grady's allegiances have completely changed, I'm glad they're here because Joanna is my best friend. It hurts my heart that our bond is slipping, but it's undeniable that we're not the same as we once were. She cares for me, but she's madly in love with Grady. And I can't possibly talk to her about how I feel about Ryne, not with everything that's happened.

And Ryne is all I think about. He consumes me, day and night. Even now, I watch the way he moves and talks to Elle, and I'm sick with jealousy. Every cell in my body craves his touch, but he's cold and distant.

We're not any safer than we were before. In fact, we're less so, but maybe that's the point. Laik doesn't want to keep Ryne and Elle safe at the expense of his people. I can't say I blame him, knowing what I do about King Thorn.

We make camp that night, and nobody talks to me, not even when I try to lay my pack down next to Ryne. He gets up and moves to the other side of camp. That one action alone is like a twisting knife to the wound, and I only get angrier at him. He thinks he's the only one who's been hurt here? What about his actions? His choices? Why do I have to be the one to extend the olive branch? Will he ever look at me with love in his eyes like he used to? I go to bed with these questions swirling in my mind and get little rest.

The next day, we walk and walk and walk, and still, nobody talks to me. I try to make small talk with Joanna, but she keeps it surface-level and then ditches me for Grady. Charlotte and Knox seem to have some kind of budding romance happening because they are practically attached at the hip and don't give me a second thought. Elle is too busy scouting the area to pay much attention to me and my hurt feelings. I could reach out to Callum, but I feel weird about it. I don't want him to think he has a chance with me because with Ryne here, there's no question.

I want Ryne back.

Maybe it's the dumbest thing I've ever wanted, but it's eating me alive, and I can't let it go on without doing something. Sure, I'm lycan, but we can work that out. I just can't kiss him again, but even to hold his hand and hug him would mean so much. I try not to let the silent treatment bother me or let them see that I care, but my heart goes from angry to aching. I'm doing the best I can, and it's not like anyone else here is perfect. We're all making mistakes left and right. It feels like whatever I do, I'm going to make someone mad, so shouldn't I do what I think is best?

When we finally stop to set up camp the next day, I nearly cry out with exhaustion and relief. After helping set up the women's tent and foraging for firewood, I follow the little stream, hoping to find a private place to bathe. I'm pretty sure I smell like a horse.

It's warm enough for me to have some time to dry off in the sun, so I find a deep pool and strip down but keep my underwear on. There are too many people who could walk up on me to be comfortable bathing naked. I take a bit of soap from my bag with clean clothes and step into the cool water. I hiss, the water colder than I thought it would be. I'm still not used to my hot lycan blood. Sinking deep into the water, I let it soothe my aching joints. I scrub at my hair and body, getting all the dirt off. My skin becomes blissfully numb, and I lay my head back on a rock to relax and just enjoy the day.

A splash jars me out of my reverie. It's followed by laughter, but I can't see anyone. I swim across the pool and peek around the corner. If I had just walked twenty feet more, I would've found a gorgeous lake surrounded by thick trees. Elle and Ryne are splashing one another, huge smiles on their faces.

I know they aren't a couple but seeing them together makes me want to cry. They belong with one another. Even fate couldn't make me and Ryne work, but they're so easy and perfect. They match--their power, their determination, their leadership. Everything. At least they're not completely naked this time, unlike the first time I caught them together right after shifting from their wolf forms. They're in their underwear, same as me.

A tear slips down my cheek. Feeling foolish, I take a step back so they can't see me.

Too late.

"Poppy," Elle calls. Ryne's back is to me, but his whole body stiffens. Elle ignores him and swims over. She grabs my hand and pulls me into the middle of the lake with them.

Ryne swims to the other side and hoists himself onto the shore. I don't even bother trying to hide my stare. He's lost a little weight--we all have out here--but he's still ripped with muscle. The water streams down his tanned skin and tangles his black hair.

"Come on, Ryne, don't be an idiot," Elle calls after him.

Ryne spins. "Idiot? Poppy tricked me and kidnapped me."

Elle rubs her eyes. "Are you sure that's what happened?"

He crosses his arms and glares at me. "Are you saying it's not?"

"No, that's exactly what happened," I say, and Ryne scowls. "But I did it to save your life."

"I'm supposed to believe that?" His natural distrust hurts, and I want to leave. It's hard enough that we're estranged now. I don't need to be reminded.

"Of course you are," Elle says with exasperation. "Now get back in here. You and Poppy have to work this out."

For a second, I think he's going to storm away, but instead he listens to Elle and slides back into the water. I wonder if he'd ever listen to me the way he does her. Probably not, but maybe that's a good thing. Elle is his friend, and friends can be real with you in ways that lovers cannot.

And I never wanted to be Ryne's friend.

He swims over to us and stands up. The water comes up to my chest, but only his torso. He glowers down at me. I feel like there's a ten-foot glass wall between us. I can't climb over it, so I'm just going to have to break it.

"You have thirty seconds to convince me that you are not my enemy."

"Wait," Elle says, backing away. "I'm going to give you guys some privacy. I'll keep watch so no one else interrupts you either."

I appreciate her optimism, but I'm not convinced it's necessary.

We both watch Elle leave the lake and disappear into the woods. I'm both grateful and nervous that she left us. Ryne could do whatever he wanted with me, and I'm not sure I'd fight him. He could kill me. Drown me right here and run away. His pack wouldn't blame him.

But he stares at me, torment clear in his eyes. I did betray him, but only because I love him. And I've realized now, that a lot of the bad choices he made when it came to me were out of love too. We're just two messy people trying to survive a horrible situation.

"That mission wasn't supposed to have anything to do with you," I begin. "We were supposed to be rescuing Elle. I thought she was your wife, not your father's. I was so angry with you even though I know I didn't have a good reason to be. I am lycan, and you can't be with me, but I still felt betrayed and abandoned." I take a deep breath and stand a little taller. I can do this. "We found you asleep, and Laik wanted to kill you." I leave the part out about Grady wanting to kill him because he's been hurt enough as it is. "Even angry with you, I didn't want you dead, so I suggested we kidnap you instead. I was supposed to lure you out. I thought maybe you'd get away or . . . I don't know what I thought. But I didn't know that kissing you would knock you unconscious."

He steps closer to me and cups my cheek with his rough hand. It's a small gesture, but it's everything to me. My toes curl into the mud, and I long to wrap myself around him. "But the second time you did," he says, his voice hardening. "You sedated me for them."

I swallow, knowing there is no way out of this. "I did. But again, I was doing the best I could to keep us both alive. I was stuck between two hard choices."

"Would you have made that same choice again knowing that I'm not married to Elle?"

"I would do anything to save you, married or not. Can't you see that?" I inch forward, spreading my hands on his bare chest. When he doesn't flinch or pull away, hope fires within me. "I still love you, and it hurts so badly that we can't be together."

He hesitates for a moment and then crushes me in a hug. "I've missed you so much," he whispers in my hair.

Tears prick my eyes, and I clutch at his back. I didn't think I'd ever hold Ryne again, but here we are in the middle of a lake, clinging to one another like there is no tomorrow.

And maybe there isn't.

Especially when Laik finds out.

Ryne drops his head and kisses my neck, trailing his lips up along my jaw and across my cheek. Everywhere his lip touch burns, and I crave more and more. No one else in the world matters except me and Ryne. Whatever happens after this, at least we will be in it together.

Then his mouth is on mine, and I open my mouth and run my tongue along his lips. A half a second later, my mind clears, and I remember that I can't kiss him. He's about to pass out in the middle of the lake. He's too big for me to carry on my own. He'll drown!

Maybe I'll kill him after all.

CHAPTER 23

I rip away from him and squeeze around his middle. "Come on," I grunt. "It's not safe here."

He chuckles. "Poppy."

I can't move him. The man is practically twice my size, and my lycan strength has waned with the moon.

"Poppy," he says again, crouching down and peeling my arms away from him. "I'm okay. I feel completely normal." He chuckles again. "Well, I do feel like I want to kiss you, but you know what I mean."

I blink at him, relief flooding me. "My kiss didn't hurt you?" I can't figure out what's changed.

He shakes his head. "But just in case, we'd better test it again."

His lips return to mine, and I want to shake him off, to tell him we should try this on the shore, but my mind blanks when he deepens the kiss. Fear of my saliva doesn't deter him or slow him down, and if anything he's more energized from kissing me. It's the validation I need. I float my legs up to wrap around his torso and press myself closer. I could stay like this forever.

"You're shivering," he says. "Let's get out of here."

We swim over to his clothes and then walk up the trail to retrieve mine.

"Laik said that lycan saliva is what poisons you, so this doesn't make any sense."

"It does," he replies. "Your bite is deadly, but only when you're in lycan form. Your saliva acts similarly to the wolfsbane. It weakens us but I don't think it's deadly."

I raise an eyebrow at him. "You don't look weak to me, and let's not forget you just had your tongue down my throat."

"When you put it that way, I don't sound very romantic, do I?" He grins sheepishly.

I snort out a laugh and shimmy into my clothes, then run my fingers through my hair in a pathetic attempt to brush it. "You know what I mean." And then it dawns on me. "Lycan are stronger the closer we get to the full moon, so that means I can't kiss you before or after it."

He smirks. "What's that? Five or six days every twenty-eight?"

"Something like that. I don't know for sure."

He wraps me in a hug. "Good thing we have plenty of time to figure it out."

"Do we?" I wish we did, but we both know what a mess we've gotten ourselves into. It feels surreal to be here, kissing and acting like lovestruck kids who have nothing to worry about but each other. But that's not our reality, and I'm not sure it ever will be.

"Maybe not, so we'd better make the most of it while we still can."

That's all I needed to hear to meet his lips again and pick up where we left off out in the lake. Too bad we don't have more privacy here and have to resort to making out in the woods, but at this point, I'll take whatever I can get. I want Ryne. I love him. And lycan or not, he's my fated mate. We'll figure the details out later.

Someone clears their throat, and we spring apart. Elle peeks her head out from behind a tree, a satisfied smirk on her pretty mouth. "Sorry to interrupt, but we have to get back before Laik sends out a search party."

I thread my fingers with Ryne's. "So what are we going to do? Do we pretend that we're not together or--" It's also my way of asking if we *are* together, but I'm not always as brave as I'd like to think.

"They're not keeping us apart anymore," he replies quickly.

"They could use our status against us."

"Like I said..." He squeezes my hand. "They're not keeping us apart anymore." I appreciate his confidence, but I'm not so sure we can pull it off.

"They don't trust any of us," Elle points out.

"She's right," I add. "At the very least, we can't let them know that we're fated." That's dangerous knowledge even in the hands of friends. In the hands of enemies, it's deadly.

"Fine." But he doesn't sound fine. He sounds angry. "But those people kept me tied up with painful wolfsbane rope for two weeks. If they want my help, the least they can do is leave you and me alone."

I agree, but I have a sinking feeling not everyone is

going to see it the same way. Even my allies might not be so friendly about it. I shudder to think of what Joanna and Grady will say. I'm going to have to warn him about them.

Elle rolls her eyes. "You two are disgustingly cute, do you know that?"

I blush and squeeze Ryne's hand a little tighter.

"Nobody has ever called me disgustingly cute before," Ryne grumbles. We grow silent for a long second before we all burst out laughing.

* * *

We're halfway back to the camp when something zips out of the forest, tackling Ryne to the ground. My first thought is that we've been ambushed, but then I recognize the wolf with a missing limb. Grady. Despite the loss of a leg, his movements are still swift and precise. More importantly, his teeth are still razor-sharp, and right now they're clasped around Ryne's neck.

"No!" I scream, rushing forward, pulling at Grady's fur, but he's already on top of Ryne, saliva dripping onto his face. I claw and grab, but it's useless.

Elle shifts, her clothes ripping to pieces. I jump back, giving her space to help. Joanna stumbles onto the trail and grabs my hand. Tears shine on her cheeks, and her mouth is set in a grim line. "I told him not to go after you guys."

Time slows down. Grady lets go of Ryne's neck seconds before Elle collides with him. I expect Ryne to shift into his wolf, but he doesn't. Instead, Grady changes back and falls onto his knees. "Fight me!" he screams. "Turn and fight me, damn it!"

Ryne shakes his head and stands, brushing off his pants. Grady gets right into his face. "What's the matter? Are you a coward when dear old dad isn't here to instruct you?"

Grady shoves at Ryne, and he stumbles back a step but doesn't fall. I grip Joanna's arm and she mine. Elle still circles both of them in her wolf form. I've no doubt she'd take Grady down if he really hurt Ryne.

"I'm so sorry," Ryne says. "I didn't have a choice."

"There's always a choice." Underneath all that anger is the vulnerability of betrayal.

"You got out of there alive."

Grady sniffs. "Because of Poppy. Don't pretend you had anything to do with that. You would've killed me."

Ryne's eyes flick to where Grady should have an arm. Grady catches Ryne's gaze and hauls off, punching him in the jaw. Ryne's head jerks back, and I flinch. Elle stops her pacing and crouches into a fighter's stance.

Ryne recovers and rubs his jaw. "I deserved that."

"You sure as hell did."

"Are you done?"

Grady shakes his head and punches him in the gut. Ryne doubles over, and I move to go to him, but Joanna holds tight to me. "If they are ever going to get out of this as friends, we have to let them fight it out," she hisses in my ear.

"But Ryne's not fighting."

"I know. And that's okay. Grady needs this. Let him have it."

"By using Ryne as a punching bag?" I squeak just as Grady throws another punch, blood exploding from Ryne's nose.

"Please, forgive me," Ryne says, his voice thick.

Grady stands there, breathing heavily, and then gives a stiff nod. He holds his hand out, and Ryne takes it. "You were my best friend and I trusted you."

"I know."

"We'll never be friends again, but I will work with you to take down Thorn."

Ryne nods once.

"After that," Grady continues, "I don't ever want to see your face again."

Ryne's mouth thins, and his eyes soften. As much as it hurts, he gets it. Too much damage has been done.

Joanna bounces up on her toes. "I think that's the best we're going to get."

Elle shifts back, and we walk back to camp in tense silence. Well, until Elle starts chattering. She rambles on about the girls with Madame Delphine, about how she wants to help them before more get shipped off to the mating houses. Ryne keeps a tight hold of my hand, and Joanna has her hand tucked into Grady's remaining arm. He and Ryne both walk on the outside of our group, farthest away from each other, but at least they agreed they were on the same side.

Camp is noisy when we return, with lunch well underway.

We get in line for food, and the cook plops a little less on Ryne, Elle, and Grady's plates, but none of them complain. We find Knox, Charlotte, and Callum sitting on a large fallen log and join them.

Callum eyes Ryne's arm around my back but doesn't say anything. Knox won't look up from his plate. This is exactly what I was worried about. Knox told me he thinks the wolves should die, that Ryne should die. What if he tries something?

"Hey, Knox," Ryne says, and Knox barely lifts his eyes.

"Yeah?" He clears his throat. "Hi."

"Thanks for taking care of Poppy for me. I owe you one."

"I did it for Poppy, not you."

"Right," he says, "understandable."

I haven't been sure if I should tell Ryne the truth about Knox's feelings toward him or not. I don't want to get Knox into trouble for no reason. Ryne still doesn't know about our dating history, but I don't want to keep it a secret anymore. I'm tired of secrets. I'll tell him all about it once we have a chance to be alone. Surely Ryne wouldn't hold my past with Knox against him, especially since Knox doesn't have a chance with me anymore, and Knox helped me get out of the city.

"We should plan our next move," Elle declares. "The full moon is only ten days away, and you all are the strongest on those days."

"You should be talking to Laik and Wanda about that, not us," Callum replies.

Elle creases her eyebrows. "Why? Are they the only ones who can help?" She scoffs. "They're working for the Resistance, same as all of us."

Callum shakes his head. "But Laik is the alpha. We don't do anything without his permission."

Elle rolls her eyes. "He's not my alpha. I'm no lycan." She scrunches her nose. "No offense."

"You know what I mean . . ." His voice drops. "I don't do

anything unless it's okay with my alpha. That's the way it works around here."

I have a thought then--what if the alpha-hierarchy here isn't as strong as Laik wants me to believe? In the shifter pack, the wolves can change at will and are connected to each other through their senses and the telepathic link. Lycan are similar, but I've never seen the lycan here treat Laik even close to the way that Ryne's pack treated him. Maybe Laik is just a bully who calls himself an alpha because he wants power, not because he actually has it. If I'm right, it could change everything, and it could also explain why Callum just got all weird.

"Well, guess what." Elle has that knowing gleam in her eyes she gets whenever she's passionate about something. "I'm in charge of the Resistance, so he'll have to listen to me, and I value your contribution far more than Laik's."

We all stare at her, and I can't help but grin. When I met her, I really thought she'd be my enemy. Thank heavens I was so wrong.

"Why?" Callum asks.

"You're the healer, right? You have much more of a sense on how to attack with the least amount of life lost. You're safe, not reckless. I want you to be my liaison between us and the lycan, not Laik."

She winks at me, and I wonder what she's up to. Perhaps it's just that she wants to undermine Laik's authority. Or she could be telling the truth. Or she could simply have a crush on Callum. I'm kinda hoping it's the last one, as far-fetched as it could be. I've never seen her crush on anyone, but if they did get together, then maybe

Callum will talk to me like he's a friend and not a jilted lover.

"I can't do that."

"Why not?" Elle pops a wilted strawberry into her mouth and frowns.

"Because Laik is my alpha. I cannot defy him." But his voice wobbles a little, and again, I wonder how much control Laik actually has over his pack. This is an interesting development, and I can't wait to have some alone time to talk with Ryne about it.

"I'm not asking you to defy him. I'm simply asking that you be my go-between. You know Laik and I are going to have conflicts. This eases that."

Callum snorts. "For you maybe, but not for me."

"Fine, then Charlotte can be my liaison."

"Nope. Laik isn't my alpha. I barely know the guy." Charlotte holds up her hands, a half-eaten apple still in her right palm. "I can't help you with that one."

Elle looks at me.

"I didn't swear allegiance to him," I say. Beside me, Ryne's shoulders relax.

"See, Callum," Elle says. "It has to be you."

Callum twists his lips and gets up to leave, but he doesn't say no again, and I'm pretty sure Elle's got him on the hook.

CHAPTER 24

Ryne and I spend as much time together as possible over the following days, testing the strength of my kiss whenever we're alone. The moon grows a sliver larger each night, but so far we've been fine. My saliva isn't hurting him. He still has his own tent because Laik doesn't trust him to sleep near the others, and I find myself sneaking in to be with him after the other women fall asleep and returning hours later. Our romance isn't a secret, but I don't want the extra attention that moving into his tent permanently would create. We're playing a dangerous game, a game of deep kisses and blissful temptation and shifting alliances--I never want it to end.

Three days before the night of the full moon, I wake up with a sense of urgency coursing through my veins. I slip from my blankets and hurry outside to help with breakfast. Looking around, I can tell I'm not the only one here who feels what I'm feeling. There's an intensity in the air that wasn't present yesterday. Even though the lycan here have gotten along with the wolf shifters well enough, I worry that may not last as the full moon draws closer.

"There you are." Ryne drops a kiss on my cheek and wraps an arm around my waist. "How did you sleep?"

"Honestly? Great." I look up at him, and he leans in to peck me on the lips, but I duck away and step back. "But I feel different today."

"Different?"

"Charged somehow." I swallow hard. "I don't think we should kiss again until three days after the full moon. I don't want to hurt you."

He lets out a breath and nods. That's a whole week every moon cycle that we're going to have to be extra careful. It stinks, but at least it's not every day.

"What are you telling him our secrets for, huh?" Wanda strides right up to me, squaring her shoulders and getting in my face. I'm taller than her and probably a better fighter, but she's unpredictable.

"I don't know your secrets. And besides, he's on our side," I reply. "You have a problem? Take it up with Laik."

"No," Ryne interrupts. "Take it up with Elle. She's the highest-ranked here right now." I smile at him, and not for the first time, I wonder how he feels about not being the alpha. Technically he's still the alpha of his pack. They won't fight for a new one until they can sense he's dead through the pack bond, but Elle was never one of his, so she's not bound to him. She's all Resistance now, and seeing her out here is witnessing her in her element. She's an exceptional leader.

"Whatever." Wanda's tone completely changes, going

light and sweet. It would catch me off guard except that I'm used to her erratic behavior. "That might change today."

"Why do you say that?" I study her, trying to gauge if she's bluffing, but I can never tell with her.

She falls silent as Laik approaches. "We're going on a little field trip today," he announces loud enough that everyone in earshot can hear. "It's time we take this matter of Elle's disruption to the source."

"The source?" I question.

"The Resistance, you dummy." Wanda cackles. She twirls away and follows Laik over to the morning campfire.

"This should be interesting," Ryne says with a long sigh. Something lingers in his eyes. Fear? No, not fear, but he's nervous, and I can't say I blame him for that.

"Anyone who hasn't sworn loyalty to us has to wear a blindfold." Laik's eyes dart to those of us who aren't part of his little pack. We've hiked to the three trucks, and Elle's helping with seating arrangements when he decides to make this announcement.

"Oh, not this again," I mutter.

"I'm not putting that thing on," Joanna snaps.

"If you want to come, you will wear it." Laik straightens, his face stern.

"We're all part of the Resistance," Elle argues. "And haven't we already discussed this? You don't make the rules."

"But I make the rules about the safety of my camp, and I have a right to keep its location hidden."

"A little late for that, don't you think?" Grady chuckles. "Most of us know where we are, genius."

A few in the group stiffen, but most seem unfazed. Hope blooms in my chest. Maybe they're starting to realize that Laik isn't all that great.

"It's true," Joanna adds. "You're not the only one who has a strong sense of direction."

Laik growls but throws the blindfolds into the back of the closest truck. "Let's roll," he calls out before climbing into the driver's seat and slamming the door.

"We're not going in his vehicle," Joanna says, peering up at Grady. We split up, and Laik's people end up either with him or in the second truck, while the rest of us squash into the third. Knox drives with Charlotte in the cab while the wolves, Joanna, and I sit in the back. It's the closest Ryne and Grady have been to each other since their fight, and Elle eyes them carefully.

Grady sets Joanna in his lap and then whispers something in her ear. She giggles. He turns to look away from me and Ryne but keeps talking low to her. They're so often in their own little world, and I hate that I find myself jealous. I have Ryne, but it's not like we can just run away together. Grady and Joanna could. They could leave right now and never look back.

"Comfortable?" Ryne asks, his fingers sliding along the little sliver of exposed skin above my shorts.

"Not really," I laugh. "But I'm not complaining." I lean back into him and close my eyes, allowing the next hour to go by in relaxing silence. I don't even mind the bumpy war-torn roads because I've got Ryne to keep me comfortable.

* * *

The little room is packed with people. Even though my senses are slightly enhanced, I can't tell who is what. There are lycan, humans, and panther shifters all around us. Pretty sure Grady, Ryne, and Elle are the only wolf shifters, but maybe not.

Several people have poppies stuck to their shirts or in their hair.

"What's with the poppies?" I hiss to Elle.

She grins at me. "Don't you know? You're famous. The girl who stood up to King Thorn. Since you left, your namesake has become a symbol of solidarity."

I don't even know how to respond to that. Instead, I glance down at my shoes, avoiding the eyes of those around us. How many people had these boots before me? There's a small hole growing in the toe.

Elle drags us all the way to the front of the room, where Laik is talking with another man. He's tall, with bronzed golden skin even darker than the wolves, vibrant yellow eyes, and black cropped hair. He's not much older than Ryne and is stunning to look at. I can't help but wonder who he could be--someone with power, if I had to guess.

Laik glares at Ryne as we approach. "He's not leadership," he growls.

The other man ignores Laik and holds his hand out to Ryne. "Welcome, we've been waiting a long time for you to join our side. I'll admit I was skeptical, but Delphine and

Elle insisted you'd do it. I'm Derek, leader of the panther pack."

Ryne tilts his head and studies the leader. "I know who you are. Gotta say, I shouldn't be surprised to see you here, but I am."

Derek nods. "This is the closest we come to wolf territory. We aid the Resistance and nothing more."

"If my father knew--"

"War would break out," Derek finishes. "We know. And we don't want that for our people. I'm glad you're on the right side of history now."

"My mother always had more faith in me than I had in myself. Elle did too," Ryne says.

"I'm glad they did." He turns to Laik, who's got his arms folded over his broad chest, still glaring daggers at Ryne. "Come now, Laik, there is no reason to be like that. Ryne offers a unique perspective into the wolf shifter dynamics."

"Fine. Put him out there with all the other shifters. He doesn't need to be up here."

"Actually, he does," Elle says.

"Why?" Laik challenges. His nostrils flare as if he smells something vile. "We've got too many wolves here as it is."

"Because he's the one who'll have to take down his dad at some point. We can't do this without him."

The two begin a stare off, and the tension builds. Someone has to back down, or else there will be a fight any second. I've never seen Elle like this. Her leadership skills are unmatched.

"Fine," Laik growls at last, stepping back. "Let's get started."

I turn and find that Joanna and Grady aren't behind me.

I search the crowd and see them talking and laughing with another couple. Joanna doesn't laugh with me like that anymore. Callum, Knox, and Charlotte are with them as well. Maybe I shouldn't be up here either.

I extract myself from Ryne. "I'm going to go be with them."

Elle laughs. "Absolutely not. You're in this with us."

Laik opens his mouth to argue, but Derek cuts him off. "Let's get this started then, shall we?"

He steps forward, holding his hands up. It takes a few moments, but the crowd quiets. "Before we begin, I want to introduce you to some new faces up here with me. Prince Ryne Tremaine, alpha of the Carolina Pack, has finally joined us."

A cheer goes up.

"Yes, he plans to assassinate his father." The crowd silences with that declaration, and Ryne's face goes red. I can see the pain in his eyes and wonder if I'm the only one. No son should have to kill his own father, no matter how evil the father is. I wish I could take this from him, but there are too many people depending on Ryne to do the right thing. These are all things we've talked about in our time alone together the past few days, and his plan before we kidnapped him hasn't gone away. As one of the only men allowed close to Thorn on a regular basis, Ryne is committed to seeing this through.

"And we will do anything we can to help him with that," Derek continues. Everyone nods, and murmurs of agreement circle the room. He talks as if he's used to giving speeches, and he motions to me with confidence. "Standing at his side is someone you've all heard of by now. I'm honored to introduce you to Poppy."

A hush falls over the room, and red-hot embarrassment spreads across my cheeks.

"Poppy has become a symbol for our cause," he continues. "We fight for her and all the other girls she represents. She is one of the lucky ones. She was turned lycan, but she escaped Thorn's clutches. We will not rest until everyone is free from the tyranny of the wolves."

Another cheer. I still don't understand what's going on, but I let myself look at these people, meeting their eyes. They care about this as much as I do. They're committed--we're going to make this happen.

Derek waits for the crowd to quiet once more. "Before we talk about the plan for the upcoming full moon, I want updates from all of you. What have you done that has aided the Resistance? What have you seen that has weakened their stronghold? Who needs rescuing?"

Several hands shoot up all over the room, and Derek calls on them one by one. They all tell tales of things they've done and accomplished, but there are also stories of wolves who've done unspeakable things. When those stories are told, Ryne tightens his grip on my hand. I know he blames himself, and others in this room probably blame him too. But I don't blame him anymore. For a long time I did, but I know who he really is--I know his heart. It's not his fault he was born to be the alpha, but he's changing his fate, despite the odds. I admire him for that.

Once they are done, Derek waves Laik forward.

"What is the plan for the lycans on this full moon?"

"We're going to go into the city and take down as many

of those bastards as possible." He speaks like the answer is obvious and that he'll be successful. I'm not so sure.

"That's not going to work," Ryne says sharply. He rakes a hand through his hair, and his mouth thins. Everyone turns on him, and whispers ripple through the crowd.

CHAPTER 25

"Why not?" Laik growls. His fists are clenched, and I'm a little nervous he's going to attack Ryne on the spot. From the looks of it, he wouldn't be the only one.

Ryne takes it all in stride, seemingly unafraid. "Because since the last festival, they've become far more vigilant. They don't let anyone into the city on the full moon or even a few days before. And considering you kidnapped me the day after the full moon, I can only imagine security has grown tighter."

"We have ways of getting into the city undetected," Laik insists, and I have to fight to roll my eyes. Ways? We crossed a ramshackle bridge on the verge of collapse.

"Explain," Ryne says, unconvinced.

"I'm not telling you our secrets. Just know that it can be done."

Ryne furrows his brow, disbelieving.

I'm acutely aware that this conversation is happening in

front of everyone, but these two don't seem to care. They obviously hate each other, and the forced proximity is starting to wear thin.

"Whatever. Even if you can get into the city, the plan to just kill at random is a stupid one."

"Because you're protecting them."

"They're my pack!" Ryne yells, and everyone goes still. "Not every wolf is evil. I know those men. They're my brothers, and they're not in control of the laws governing our ways. Killing them serves no purpose." He takes a deep breath to steady his voice. He's got some convincing to do now, and for more than just Laik's sake. Others are starting to eye Ryne with distrust. "War is bloody, I know that, but we should avoid killing as many innocents as possible. Why not try to take out key people that are close to my father?"

"Like you?" Laik laughs.

"Not helpful," Derek mutters.

"Like Anders, and I *know* you people know how dangerous he's gotten. So start with him, and if we can also take out the ones my father brought in from Chicago, when the time comes for me to challenge him, everyone else will be on my side."

Laik grins. "Why not challenge dear old dad now? Why wait?"

I squeeze Ryne's hand because I don't want him to take the bait.

"Timing is key. I'll only get one chance, and we can't blow it."

"You're stalling."

"My father is a fearsome fighter, and I'm not as strong

as I need to be. Since I arrived at the lycan camp, I've felt weak. You kept me locked up and malnourished until Elle arrived with some common sense." He gives Laik a pointed look. "I need another month, if not more, to regain my strength and prepare."

"Are we going to allow the lycan into the city when Ryne challenges Thorn?" I ask. I'm so caught up in the conversation that I don't even realize I've spoken. But I'm worried about Ryne. He could die. And if they do it on the full moon, I'm not sure I'll even be aware of what's going on. I need to be there when it all goes down, just in case there's a way I can help.

Derek speaks up. "I think we should. And as much as I hate to say this, the panthers may break the treaty to be there as well. At that point, we want to make sure the wolves have the leadership we put in place, not their own. The Resistance needs to subdue them."

Ryne shifts uncomfortably, and I can't say I blame him. We don't know these panthers, and they could hurt his people. But at the same time, we may need their help.

"But how will you know who the good guys are?" I ask. "Because not all the wolf shifters are bad."

"That is a conversation for another time. For tonight, we should focus on who the lycan should target this month. I agree with Ryne. Taking them out randomly is counterproductive and too risky." Derek raises an eyebrow. "Let's make a plan."

The conversation changes as new strategies are outlined, but it's Laik who's got my attention. The man can't be trusted, and it's only a matter of time before he lashes out.

Over the next hour, our plans all start to come together like storm clouds gathering. If everything works, we'll be successful. We're almost through when someone enters the room. She's breathing hard, like she's been running, and she has a black cloak over her head. "Sorry I'm late," she says, removing the hood. It's Madame Delphine.

Her eyes lock on Ryne, and then she's rushing through the crowd and climbing onto the stage to wrap her son into a tight hug. "I knew you were alive, but I was so worried."

"I'm okay." They pull apart and smile at each other. It's one of the rare times I get to see them as mother and son, and it makes my heart ache for them both. Their relationship should be simple, but Thorn has made it complicated.

"I have news," she announces to everyone. "And I don't have much time, so please let me say my peace."

Derek nods, and she begins. "There was a plan to bring more betas into the claiming this year so that more of the claimed women could become beta wives. That, unfortunately, hasn't happened."

Ryne's eyes darken. "Thorn's doing?"

She nods. "I'm afraid so, but it's more than that." She swallows hard. "As you know, Anders is running the pack in Ryne's absence. Things are grim, and now he's decided that at the festival next month, more than two girls will be taken to the mating houses."

"How many more?" I breathe. There's not even that many left.

"Eight women."

"Eight!" Elle gasps. "That can't be!"

"I'm afraid it is." Madame Delphine's voice wobbles. "I

can't stay for long. I'm lucky I was able to travel here at all. There are more patrols than ever, and I need to get back before my absence is noted, but I had to come beg you to save these women."

"We'll do our best," Derek replies.

"I need you to promise. Send some of your best people to Drayton Hall on the coming full moon, and I'll help you get the most vulnerable women out."

"It will spread our resources too thin," Laik interrupts. "We already have a plan."

"I don't care about your plan." She glares at him. "This Resistance is about helping the women, is it not? Well, I'm telling you that these girls need us."

"They all need us," Laik snaps. "Every single woman in that city needs us."

He has a point, but I know those women and was friends with a few of them. And even though I wasn't close with most of them, they still don't deserve to be taken to the mating houses. I wouldn't wish that on anyone; not even Faye with all her nasty comments and sabotaging actions. Nobody deserves to go to a mating house. Nobody!

I think of Abi then. I want to get her out too. I wonder where she is now. Could I find her? Could I save her? Is it too late?

Of course it's not too late. Part of me feels guilty that I think only of her and not all the other women as well. How many of them are trapped in those hellholes? This has to stop. All of it. But if we try too much at once, we will never succeed. The Resistance isn't big enough to take the whole system down quickly.

"Laik is right that they all need us," I say. Everyone stops arguing and looks at me. I swallow and lick my lips. "But how many mating houses are there? If we try to rescue the mating house women all at once, we will fail. However, we can prevent some women from the horrors of those places to begin with if we start with the claimed. The ultimate goal is to end this inhuman practice once and for all, but right now, we have enough resources to take out a couple of key players and rescue those girls."

Laik crosses his arms and glowers at me. "And then what?"

"And then we keep doing this until we save them all."

Madame Delphine beams and squeezes my shoulder. "I knew you were going places."

"I want to help with the rescue efforts," Ryne says.

Laik practically growls. "Absolutely not. I have a few guys who are good at rescue missions. We'll send them."

Ryne's eyeballs just about pop out of his head. "Are you insane? You want to send lycan after them on a full moon? They'd be totally out of control."

"Give my alpha some credit," Wanda calls out, her voice shrill above the others. "We've gotten women out of there on full moons before. We can control ourselves just fine."

Ryne wraps a protective arm around me. "How do you explain Poppy then?"

Laik considers this for a second, and something tickles at the back of my mind--a suspicion that he's not being completely honest with us.

"I'm not saying people don't get in the way and sometimes end up bitten, which is what happened with Poppy, but if there are shifters around, my men will be able to take them on better than anyone else. One bite from us, and they won't be strong enough to fight us off."

"I'll go with them," Elle volunteers. "That way Ryne can go with the group to take out the shifters. He can identify them for you."

"No. No shifters," Laik says. "I'm not working with wolves."

"Me too," I say, ignoring Laik's obvious prejudice. "I'm coming too."

"No," both Laik and Ryne say at the same time. I huff and cross my arms. I hate that the one thing they agree on is against me.

"Why not? I know these women. They might listen to me."

Ryne snorts. "Doubtful."

"Why can't I go?"

Laik eyes me like I'm stupid. "It's only your second full moon. You aren't going to have much more control than you did on your first."

He has a point, but I can't accept it. "So we'll go in before the moon fully rises. Please."

"No. I will put my foot down on this. You will stay with the shifters, and the lycan left back at camp will help you through your renewal. Charlotte is good for that. You'll need to help Knox as well."

Ryne stiffens, and I wonder if he knew that Knox had been bitten and that I was the one who did it.

"Fine. I'll stay behind." But I don't like it. Not one bit. I'm certain I can control myself. I want to go, but now is not the place to discuss this.

"I'm still going," Elle argues.

"I told you, no shifters." Laik's voice booms as if he gets the final word.

Ryne simply ignores him. "I'm with Elle on this one. We're not sitting this out."

"This is not a democracy."

Madame Delphine steps forward. "You're right. It's not. Lest you forget, I'm the one in charge, and those are my girls you're talking about. Ryne stays back at camp with Poppy." She gives him a pointed look. "I'm sorry, son, but half the shifters are out looking for you. You going puts this whole operation in jeopardy. Elle will lead the lycans to rescue the girls. She knows Drayton Hall, and I trust her. More importantly, the claimed trust her." She turns to Elle. "Get as many as you can."

"I will," Elle nods.

I want to push my case, but at least Elle gets to go. And I have to admit, I'm glad Ryne isn't going to be in danger, but can I really just stay back? I'm going to turn into my lycan self for the second time, and I don't want to do it in front of him--not before I can learn to control it, and especially not before I've accepted myself as this new monster.

But I still want to help the women back at the manor. I'll just have to figure out a more creative way to do it.

CHAPTER 26

I wake the morning of the full moon sprawled out on Ryne's chest. He has his own tent since none of the lycan want to sleep next to a shifter, and last night I snuck out of the women's tent to be with him. I didn't plan to sleep in here, but I couldn't bring myself to leave the warm blankets or the comfort of his body. We couldn't kiss, so we spent the night cuddling and talking until we fell asleep. I study him now, taking in the sharp edges of his cheeks and chin, the dark hair fanning his pillowcase, and the fullness of his perfect lips. I want to lean up and kiss him, but I know that's a bad idea. Ryne needs to be at his full strength, and I'm pretty sure my saliva today would knock him out for days.

I settle for pressing myself as close to him as I can. These moments feel fleeting, and I wonder how long it is before we are separated again. I shouldn't worry about that. It doesn't seem like there is any reason we would be torn apart now, but based on everything that has happened so far, I don't think our luck will hold.

I keep my cheek pressed against his chest as it moves up and down with the rise and fall of his breath. It's long and slow. He's still asleep.

All of my senses are heightened, and I inhale Ryne's woodsy scent. It's my favorite smell in the whole wide world.

I smile at the thought of what Joanna would say if she heard the mushy thoughts in my head. She'd be mortified. Or maybe not? She's as in love as I am. My smile falls because I can't talk to her about this kind of thing anymore. We barely talk at all now that Ryne is no longer tied up. Before she and Grady were almost killed, I could've sat in our room and droned on and on about Ryne. She would've thrown a pillow at me, but she'd have still listened and offered advice.

Even though I get to see her every day, I miss her.

Ryne's arm tightens around me, and his breath changes.

"Morning, beautiful," he mumbles.

I prop my head up so I can look at him. "Good morning. I love you." The words seem so small compared to how I feel about him. But it still feels amazing to say it, and I want to keep repeating it over and over for the rest of my days.

"I love you too." He grins. My heart flutters, and I can't help but match his grin. I'll never tire of him. Never. "I would kiss you, but . . ."

"Yeah. I know."

He presses his lips against my forehead. "But I can kiss you in other places."

Then he moves his lips to my cheeks, the line of my jaw, down my neck . . . I shiver.

The tent flap flies open, and I jump back. "Time to get up," Elle says with way too much cheer for this time of day. She stops dead when she sees us and giggles. "I didn't think you guys could do that kind of thing today."

"We were testing the limits," Ryne growls.

Elle plops herself down on the bed. The woman has no shame. "Whatever, Laik is in a foul mood and wants everyone out there to go over the plan again. I have no idea what else there is to do. Everything seems pretty straightforward."

"I hate that I have to stay behind while you all head right into the middle of danger. What if something happens to one of you, and I'm not there?" I whine. "I'll forever feel guilty."

"Don't." Elle clasps my hand and squeezes gently. "You're still too unpredictable. You could just as easily kill us. You're safer away." She drops my hand to pat Ryne's leg. "Besides, someone's got to look after this one. An alpha without his pack is never a good thing."

Ryne groans and shakes his head. "You could say that again."

Guilt eats away at me because I haven't asked many questions about how he's doing. I've been so wrapped up in being together again that I forgot how hard this must be for him. He's got to be sick with worry. I've been around enough wolves to know they're not all bad. I think of Justin and Nico and hope they're okay. I wonder what women they're courting now and how the claiming is going for them. Given the circumstances, I can't imagine anyone is having fun, but maybe I'm wrong.

We spend our day moving our camp closer to the city. I hate that we keep having to move it, but I understand the reasoning. It's exhausting work, and by the time we're done, the afternoon is waning, and supper is on. Soon, most of our group will leave. Charlotte and Callum are staying back to make sure Knox and I handle the transition okay. I can feel the moon tugging on me and remember what it was like last month when the fever took hold. The day is already hot, and I worry Knox must be blistering, but when I ask him about it, he assures me he feels fine. He's been taking Callum's herbs, so maybe he's okay. I'm still not sure how I'm going to do tonight and Knox must be freaking out.

I give him a skeptical look. "Are you sure? Because--"

"I said I'm fine," he sighs. "I asked Laik for this, remember? It's what I want." He gives me a hard look, the kind that tells me not to ask any more questions, and he stomps off into the woods.

"Don't take it personally," Ryne says, coming up to wrap his arms around me from behind. "He's still mad that you didn't choose him."

I freeze at those words. We haven't talked about my connection to Knox because I didn't want there to be any unnecessary drama. I turn around in his arms and look into his eyes. "What do you know about us?"

He nods once. "That you were together before he was claimed."

"How did you find out?"

"After I took an interest in you, I did what I could to learn about your past. I found out you and Knox came from the same village, and the way he talked about you made it obvious. I wish you would've told me, but I understand why you didn't."

"Are you mad?"

"No. It happened before you met me. I can't blame you for that, and anyway, Knox is a good kid. I like him."

"You really think he's mad that I didn't choose him?" But I think Ryne's probably right. "Actually, don't answer that. It doesn't matter. He's moving on anyway."

"Already has." Ryne grins. "I saw him making out with Charlotte yesterday. They're probably in the woods doing it again right now."

I snort, and my cheeks redden, but I'm happy for them. Charlotte's not my favorite person, but I don't think she'd do anything to hurt Knox. She's had a crush on him for years, and if a relationship with her makes him happy, then more power to them both.

"I want to talk to you about something." I step back and hope this comes out right. "I don't want to spend time together tonight."

He frowns. "Do you think I'm ashamed to be with you when you're a lycan? I'm not."

"No, I don't think that, but I'm not ready for you to see this new side of me." My voice cracks, and my eyes water. "I'm sorry. I think I just need to do this one alone. I'm afraid I might hurt you."

He swallows hard. "Okay. I can give you that. But can you promise me that you'll try next month?"

I wish I could promise him that, but I can't. If I'm totally out of control, I still can't risk it. "I don't know," I mumble. "Let me think about it, okay?"

He gives me a frustrated look and Elle skips over to give us both a hug. "We're heading out. The moon will be rising before we know it."

She's right. I can feel it reaching out to me, a promise of what's to come. Over the next twenty minutes, the camp comes back together, and everyone gets what they need for the mission. It's a flurry of activity, and then it's silent all at once after they leave. There's just me, Ryne, Charlotte, Knox, and Callum. We're the leftovers, and we know it.

"We're going to spend the evening in the medic's tent if you need us," Callum says, and they leave me and Ryne standing around aimlessly.

"This is weird," I say. I suck my lip between my teeth and rock back on my heels.

"I think it's great." His smile quirks, and he runs his fingertips along my arm. "Alone time."

I shake my head. "I think I need to start *my* alone time now. I'm sorry."

His face falls, but he understands and retreats to his tent. I hightail it out of there, my heart pounding in my chest and guilt eating at me for the second time today.

I lied to Ryne.

This isn't about me needing to be alone, even though I don't want him to see me change--I don't know if I'll ever be ready for that--no, this is about me needing to go after Elle and the lycan in her group. I can't let them go to Drayton Hall without me. What if something happens?

And what if my help could get one more girl out of there? I know that manor better than any of those lycan, and if they're not willing to let me come along for the ride, then I'll just have to invite myself.

CHAPTER 27

I keep to the woods as I head toward Drayton Hall. If I can find the river, then I can find the manor. I'm surprised by how easily I know the way, but with my heightened senses, it's second nature. I can practically smell it from here--smell the bread rising in the kitchen, the flowers growing out front next to the large garden, and the lavender and vanilla scented soap in the bathrooms. This is unlike anything I've experienced before, and I haven't even completed the shift yet. What will it be like my second time as a lycan? I need to hurry because I don't plan on that happening until after I'm away from the manor, just in case I lose control again.

It doesn't take me long to catch up with the rest of the group. I can see and smell them, but my scent is probably mixed in with everyone else's because nobody looks my way. I stay several hundred yards back, unmoving as I watch them from behind a thicket of trees. They are waiting on the river's edge for the moon to rise. I'm going to have to swim--as are they--but I'm sure I can manage it. The river is gentler here than in other parts, and lycan are stronger than the current. The girls won't like being dragged through water, but they'll survive, and eventually, they'll be thanking us.

I keep an eye on the darkening sky. I'd say we have maybe twenty or thirty minutes until they get the girls. I push my hearing out over the trickling of water and the brushing of wind against trees, landing on the manor. I can hear the girls hustling down into the basement, footsteps and nervous voices. If I try hard enough, I can even hear the faint pattering of their hearts.

This ability is astonishing.

Madame Delphine is going to intentionally leave their door unlocked, but how will that work without casting suspicion on her? I've seen that lock. It's huge. Maybe she'll open it when it's dark. Maybe she'll create a diversion.

I hope we can trust her. What if we're walking into a trap? Madame Delphine wouldn't do that, would she?

I swallow and try to stay grounded. The plan is for each of the lycan to grab two girls and run off with them. Meanwhile, Elle will go after four girls who are more likely to want to escape the city. I'll stay in the background and keep an eye on the lycan with girls. I don't want there to be any accidental bites, and deep down I know I could hurt someone. It's better that I stay back and watch. I'll help if they need me, but hopefully they won't.

The moon continues to rise, and I feel myself change. It happens faster than it did the first time. I fall to my knees, keenly aware that this life isn't what I wanted. My senses grow even stronger, and I'm suddenly thirsty. It's not water

I need. It's human flesh. But my mind is still clear enough for me to push that horrible need away. If I get to the point that I'm close to losing control, I'll force myself to run.

My hands elongate, and thick nails form. They're like little daggers, pressing into the dark soil. My shoulders broaden with audible pops, and my face contorts and twists. I want to scream, to howl, but I refuse to let myself. It's still painful, but not as painful as last time.

I can do this.

I can do this.

I can do this.

I get back up and stand there for a second, breathing in and out. It takes a minute of concentration, but I still seem to have my whole mind. If I were human, I'd cry with relief right about now. Instead, I take a deep, steadying breath, and the scent of two lycan and Elle slide into my awareness. Elle smells horrible, like wet dog and old tomatoes. The other wolves smell similar to Elle but fainter, and the girls smell like the copper of human blood mixed with the scent of the lavender soap. Madame Delphine had said she would try to avoid having betas protecting the hall, but she might not be successful. All I can hope is that those wolves I smell aren't powerful fighters. I don't want to injure anyone, or be injured myself . . . or die. That's always a possibility too. This is the start of a war, or maybe it's the middle or the end. I don't know, but blood has been shed and will continue to be until this is finished.

One of the lycan whips around, and I drop to the ground. He sniffs and eyes the area where I am, but I don't think he can see me.

"What's wrong?" Elle asks. She's still in her human

form, but I'm not sure why she asked one of the lycans anything. It's not like he can talk to her in this form.

He paces around the circle, eyes trained in my direction.

Elle merely stands there. How can she be so calm when she knows that it would be so easy for them to kill her? One bite, and she'd be a goner. She must trust them more than I do. Or she's just braver than I've ever been.

The lycan continues to look in my direction as they wait. A howl comes from the woods on the other side of the house. The wolves standing guard outside Drayton Hall take off after it.

It's time.

I keep my distance, but no one is paying attention to me now. Elle and the others take to the water, swimming so swiftly they're back out within seconds. It might be a good thing--the water will help cover their scents. They rush to Drayton Hall, lines of black and gray and white cutting through the night. They enter the manor quickly, wrenching open the front door, and a few seconds later, a chorus of screams ring out. The lycan appear with two girls each under their massive arms. I can't tell who the girls are, but they're all screaming and crying loudly. The guards are going to hear them and come running.

I don't see Elle or the other girls, but I'm not all that worried about them. Elle may have run from Thorn, but those women like her and won't want to hurt her. The lycan men pass by me, their fur dripping wet and clawed feet covered in grass and mud, and one of the girls manages to wriggle free. The lycan snaps at her, wrapping a grimy paw around her tiny waist. If he's not careful, he's going to bite her. I can smell her from here and know he must smell that delicious scent as well. Just because we have our wits about us doesn't mean our instinct isn't to bite and feed.

Out of nowhere, a wolf collides with the lycan, and two girls go flying. I'm pretty sure that's a beta, but which one? My eyesight is perfect in the dark, and I quickly recognize Justin's dusty-colored wolf. I hope he doesn't get bit. I'd feel terrible if something happened to him, but I know the lycan won't hesitate to shred him to pieces.

I can't sit here and let them kill Justin.

The other lycan rushes away, and I dash from the privacy of the woods and into the open meadow. I have a choice to make. I can go after the girls or help the beta. But if I help Justin, the people back at camp will kill me. Laik would never understand why I saved a beta over one of his men. Another wolf shows up--one I don't recognize--and engages the lycan in battle. The fighting turns fierce, and the girls are all but forgotten. They start to run back to the house. If I join the fight, they'll get away and likely be sent to a mating house after this.

Girls it is.

I expect my body to feel awkward, but it doesn't. My mind is clear, and I know just what to do. Within seconds, I've reached the girls. I grab one and then the other with no hesitation. There are more women out here but they're in the water and swimming for their lives. I can't possibly go after them and hold on to the ones I've got. I want to save more women, but two is better than zero.

I run faster than I've ever run before, holding my prize in my arms and dodging trees and fallen logs as we go.

They fight back but I'm far stronger and bigger than they are. One reaches up and grabs a fistful of hair, yanking hard. I howl with pain, and she lets go. I wonder if my howl hurts her ears. I don't really care. If I could just talk to them, they'd go with me willingly. If they knew who I was, they'd thank me. Maybe we could even go back and get more girls out.

But I'm stuck in this monstrous body.

I'm only seconds away from the rendezvous point, and once I get there, others will swoop in to get us all to safety. The girls continue screaming and clawing and crying, but I've got this.

Elle is already there with her two girls, as is the other lycan with one other claimed woman. I'm so glad Elle got out of the house that I don't even bother to hide my identity. I drop the ones I saved at her feet, and Elle meets my eyes.

"You weren't supposed to come," she says with a raised eyebrow.

I'm surprised she recognizes me because she's never seen me in this form before, but then again, she knows me well. I'm not the type to stay back and let everyone else handle the important work. I grunt at her, not wanting the claimed to know who I am. I'm not ready for that. I'm still hyper aware of their scents, but I don't have a desire to bite any of them. I hadn't expected to be so in control on my second renewal. It's a good thing though, or I would've done something dumb.

We only managed to save five claimed girls. Four cry when they see Elle, thanking her for saving them and seemingly bewildered that the lycan aren't planning to eat them, that we're actually here to help. One of the girls I grabbed, however, jumps up and tries to run away.

Elle latches onto her wrist, jerking her back. "It's not safe back there."

"Yes, it is, and you can't stop me." The girl turns, clawing at Elle's hand, and I finally catch sight of her face.

I've rescued Faye.

CHAPTER 28

We go back to the camp and wait for morning. When it comes, Laik tells everyone to wash up and pack because we need to move out.

Again.

I head over to the women's tent to help. Laik stops me, pressing his finger into my sternum until I stumble back. "I should leave you here," he threatens. "How dare you disobey orders."

I want to argue, to explain my reasoning, but that will only get me in more trouble. "I'm sorry. It won't happen again," I say.

He looks me up and down. "It's been another month, you know. Are you ready to swear your allegiance to me?"

"My allegiance is to the Resistance." I choose my words carefully. "And that includes you."

It's a round-about way of giving him respect without

control. He's not my alpha, and he never will be. Let him think what he wants.

He studies me for a second and then whispers low. "I saved your life, and this is how you repay me? Embarrass me again, and see what happens."

He stalks off, and I try to forget his threats while I pack. I'm dead tired and would rather our camp stay put so we can rest, but I know it's not a good idea. We're playing with fire here. It's only a matter of time before we're found by the wolf pack and attacked. We have their alpha and five of their prized women. Everyone except for Faye seems happy with our circumstances. They do as they're told, eager to get away. Charlotte promises to take them to The Sanctuary in the panther city.

"I'm not going to some sanctuary." Faye turns her nose up at Charlotte, and everyone watches her like she's lost her mind. Maybe she has.

"It's a safe place," Elle assures her. "You don't have to marry anyone or be forced to have anyone's babies. You won't be bit. You'll get to start a new life."

She shakes her head adamantly. "I don't want it. I want to go back to the manor. I had a life there. I was going to be a beta wife!"

Laik strides up to her, getting in her face. "You will do as you are told."

"And who are you to tell me what to do?" She scrunches her nose up. "You're a dirty lycan."

His lip curls, and he strikes her to the ground. I've never seen him hit a woman before.

Elle shoves him back. "Don't you dare touch her!"

Everyone is watching now, and I catch Ryne inching closer. The expression on his face is livid, but the last thing he needs to do is get involved in this quarrel.

"Let her stay with us," I interject, inwardly wanting to kick myself. What am I thinking? I should want her gone. She's never been a friend to me. "Faye can stay with us in the wilds for a while. I'm sure that after a few weeks out here, she'll be begging to go to The Sanctuary."

Faye scowls at me but doesn't say anything, and I wonder why she's suddenly grown quiet. Maybe she's scared of Laik.

"Fine," Laik relents. "But I don't want to hear another word from this ungrateful brat until she changes her attitude."

I can't say I blame him for that. "What about the rest of the plan?" I change course. "Did the Resistance take out any key players? Did any wolves die?"

At first I think he won't say, but he finally shakes his head and storms off. I guess we weren't all that successful.

I don't stick around after that. I'm covered in dirt from the night before and wearing random, ill-fitting clothing that I dug out of the women's tent early this morning. I'm dying to get clean so I hurry over to the stream, walking a ways up so I can have some privacy. Once I'm sure I'm alone, I undress and dip into the icy water to wash the lycan from my body. I've been living out here in the wilds for two months now, and I'm growing weary of it. I look down at my body though, admiring it in a new way. I've lost some fat, gained some muscle, dealt with dirt and sweat in every pore, and transformed from human to lycan twice now. I'm so much stronger than I ever thought I could be.

And I'm so ready to be done.

Then I remember the wolf city. I remember Abi and all the other humans who still need my help. This war is just getting started.

"We need to talk." Faye appears beside me, kicking a splash of water in my face. "Right now."

I glare at her. She's the last person I want to deal with. Of all the girls we could've rescued, I can't believe my luck that she's the one I brought back. Her face is still an angry red where Laik hit her. I almost feel bad for her, but she was saved when others weren't, and here she is still causing drama.

"Can I at least get dressed, or do you want to stare at my naked, shivering body?"

"Oh please, spare me the agony. Get dressed, but don't you dare go anywhere."

I climb out of the water and yank on my pants and shirt, Faye not taking her eyes off of me.

"What do you want?" I ask.

"Take me back. I was top of the leaderboard, and Justin had already promised to marry me. I've met his parents and everything. You ruined my future."

I squeeze water out of my hair. "I saved you from an unimaginably horrible future. After this, you get to *choose* who you marry. Not be forced into it by people who don't even know you."

She crosses her arms and stalks closer to me. "What if I choose Justin?"

I want to tell her that she's not Justin's first choice and that she's not good for him, but I don't. "You and I both know that things at Drayton change quickly. You could just as easily end up in a mating house or married to someone like Thorn. Look at Elle."

"And whose fault is that? Elle would be married to Ryne right now if not for you. And I would be planning my wedding. You are the one ruining everything, not the wolves."

I close my eyes and think. She's not being rational at all. Then again, Faye never has been. "Whatever. At this point, it's not my choice. Do yourself a favor and stay out of Laik's way. Honestly, it would be better if you went to The Sanctuary. Charlotte can take you there."

"No. I'm not going to The Sanctuary, and I'm not staying here. I'm going back to Drayton Hall, and you're going to help me."

She's being ridiculous. I shove past her and head back toward the camp. She grabs my arm, jerking me back. Without thinking, I use my free hand to shove her away. It breaks her grip easily, and she flies back, landing in the water.

Oops. I forgot my own strength.

She sputters, climbing back out. "You filthy rotten lycan bitch," she yells at me. I smirk and continue walking away.

"They don't know about you and Ryne," she yells.

I spin and stare at her. She's dripping wet, a few feet behind me. "Of course they know about me and Ryne. We share a tent half the time, not that it's any of your business. They're all used to us being a couple."

"But I bet they don't know you're fated mates." She pauses to gauge my reaction, an eyebrow lifting in satisfaction. "They'd never let you stay together. They can't trust you to do what's best for the group when you'll always choose each other."

I have a feeling Laik already suspects, but he hasn't said anything. Ryne and I have been very careful to keep it a secret because she's right. If the others knew for sure, who knows what they'd do. They may kill us or use that knowledge to their advantage. Blackmail wouldn't be off the table--they could hurt me to get Ryne to do just about anything they want. Being his fated is the most wonderful feeling—I wouldn't trade it for the world, but it's also dangerous.

I can't have her blabbing.

"Faye. I know you're pissed, but this is low. You can't tell them."

"Take me back to Justin, or I will."

She's serious. I know she's beautiful, but Justin doesn't seem like the type to go for the mean girl, and I really doubt they're going to be together in the end. Then again, Faye has a way of getting what she wants, and it's been two months since I left. The summer is half gone, and I know all too well how much can change in a season.

"Fine," I relent. "Let me talk to Ryne, and we'll figure out a way to get you back."

She snorts. "Oh no. You can't talk to him."

"Why not?"

"Because he'll want to find a way to keep me away from them. He ran away, right? He betrayed his own pack. He's not going to bring me back to them."

"Actually, he was kidnapped and hasn't been allowed to return yet. He cares about his men, and if Justin really loves you, Ryne will find a way to make sure you guys are together."

Faye's face falls for a nanosecond. There's something there, like insecurity or sadness, but it's gone before I can be sure. "Fine. Talk to Ryne, but don't tell him it's because I threatened you."

I doubt I'll keep that information to myself. Ryne and I have been telling each other everything lately.

"If he sabotages this at all," she adds, "I will make sure Laik knows exactly what's going on between the two of you."

I groan, nodding. It's the best I'm going to get. "Done. Give me a couple of days, and I'll let you know our plan. Laik is intense, and he doesn't like wolves or anyone who he suspects sympathizes with them, so don't be surprised if he does what he can to prevent us from talking. But I will get you back to Justin. You have my word."

She must take that as good enough because she stalks past me, shoulder-checking me in the process. I roll my eyes and groan, wishing I could get the upper hand in this situation, but I don't see how that's possible. She's got the dirt on me and doesn't care about anyone but herself.

I hurry to finish cleaning up and follow her out of the forest. We arrive back at camp, and all the girls from the night before are sitting at a table eating breakfast. The camp is almost packed up, and I'm sure we'll be leaving in a few minutes. We've saved Faye, her friend Blair, Alyssa, Bailey, and Harlow. I don't want anyone to end up in the mating houses, but I'm glad we were able to get these women out, especially Bailey. She's got a kind heart and is super smart, but she hadn't been progressing well with the betas. I want to go to the girls and see how they are doing, but I wonder how many will see me as the enemy now.

Faye plops herself down between Blair and Alyssa, and they immediately put their heads together and whisper. Elle sits across from them with a massive smile on her face. She sees me and waves me over.

Bailey scooches closer to Harlow so I can sit between her and Elle. All the girls stop talking and stare at me.

"What?" I ask.

"You're a lycan," Bailey whispers.

"So?" I meet each of their eyes with a challenge. "I think we all know now that wolves like Thorn and Anders are the enemy, not the lycans who rescued you last night."

"We all saw what Charlotte did though," Harlow adds. She shoots a look over to where Charlotte and Knox are eating together. Guilt is written all over Charlotte's face as she watches us from afar.

I don't want to defend Charlotte, but I can't help it. "Charlotte made horrible mistakes, but she didn't mean to kill anyone, and she has control now. Really, you can trust the lycan. We're not all bad."

Faye eyes Laik on the other side of the camp. "Says you," she snaps. And she's right.

"I'm still me every other day but on the full moon, and even then, I'm still pretty much me. The first time I shifted was rough, but last night I had control. I'd never hurt anyone."

The women exchange skeptical glances, and Bailey thumps the table. "Thanks for rescuing us. I was bound for the mating house, and now I get to go to a sanctuary. I'm so excited."

That perks the others up, and they nod in agreement. Part of me is a little sad they are leaving.

"I'm not going to that sanctuary," Faye bites back. "I already talked to the boss, and he's going to let me help with the Resistance."

Elle's eyes widen skeptically, and I have to force myself to keep quiet.

"Are you sure?" Alyssa asks. "Maybe I should stay back too."

"No," Elle interjects. "You're going to The Sanctuary. Don't follow Faye's example. Faye, I don't think you should stay either. I'm going to talk to Laik. Life with the lycans is dangerous. You're much safer with the panthers."

Faye rolls her eyes. "That's funny coming from you, considering you're here with them, and one bite could kill you."

"But I'm here for a bigger cause." Elle's eyebrows knit together. "Why would you knowingly put your life in danger?"

"Because I'm not a coward. I can fight just as well as you and Poppy."

"Me too," Blair pops off. "I want to stay and help."

I open my mouth to say something, but Elle interrupts. "I'm head of the Resistance here, and I'm putting my foot down. No one stays unless they are a shifter or lycan."

Faye smirks at her, twirling a lock of her auburn hair around her finger like she knows something the rest of us don't. "We'll see about that."

Then she storms off.

I'm actually hoping that she can't convince Laik to let her stay until she goes back to Justin. But she doesn't go to Laik.

She goes to Ryne.

CHAPTER 29

In the end, Faye is the only claimed girl who sticks around. Elle was livid when she found out that Ryne and Laik both gave permission for her to stay. She argued with them for well over an hour but didn't get her way. It seems that nobody has as much power as they think they do around here, not even Elle. Ryne won't talk to me about what Faye said, but I'm sure she made similar threats to Ryne as she did to me. Of course he gave in. He's not willing to risk my life, same as I'm not willing to risk his. But why would Laik keep a snarky human girl around for no reason? He must have plans for her.

I'd take any of the other claimed girls over Faye, but they all left for The Sanctuary the next day while the rest of us moved camp again. And a week later, we moved again. And a week after that, same story. It's time we make a change because we can't keep living like this.

Until then, I'm enjoying Ryne as much as I can.

Our tent is small but perfect for the two of us. Humid

summer air keeps us warm instead of the blankets we've opted to lie on top of, and he's opened a corner of the door so that we can gaze at the stars. We can see out, but it's dark enough that nobody else can see in. We're in our own little world. After the camp's last move, I gave up sleeping in the women's tent altogether to stay with Ryne. That was the first night we felt safe kissing again, and the night we took our relationship to the next level. It was gentle and perfect at first, and then it was more. So much has changed in such a short amount of time, but it also feels like I've been with him forever.

He trails his finger across my cheek, over my shoulder, and then down to his favorite places, sending lustful shivers through my body. I lean over and kiss him, and he smiles into my lips, pressing me to my back and covering me with his warmth. I'm a changed woman because of my mate. I always knew I would make love someday, but I never expected it to be so special. It's all-consuming--claiming my emotions, my body, and my very soul. He tells me it's the same for him. He looks at me like I'm the only woman in the world, touches me like nobody else exists, and confesses he'll die if he can't have me.

Tender kisses turn frantic, and I give into the blissful heat of our flesh.

Sometime later, I'm tucked under his arm. We're still and quiet, our bodies sated and our minds at ease. It's peaceful, but that peace ebbs as my thoughts return to our issues in camp. We're wasting so much time in the wilds, and as much as I want to stay cocooned in this tent with Ryne, we have a bigger mission. The longer he's away from his pack, the more people are going to need us, but he's stuck here playing house with me and keeping Laik happy.

"You need to be the alpha," I whisper to him.

"I am the alpha."

"That's not what I mean." I roll toward him and squeeze his bicep. "I'm talking about your father. I'm talking about Chicago. You need to be the King Alpha and we can't keep stalling it from happening."

He swallows hard and nods. "I know. I've known for a long time what I have to do, but it doesn't make it any easier."

"I can't imagine what you're feeling." I kiss his warm cheek and breathe him in for a minute. I wish there was something I could do to make this all simple, but there isn't. If we're going to make changes, we have to kill Thorn soon.

"His death isn't the end of it, you know," Ryne says. "Once he's gone, there will be a massive battle for his throne."

"It doesn't automatically go to you?" I thought it was implied, but I guess I shouldn't be surprised. These wolves are used to fighting to the death.

"That's not how it works. I'll have to go to Chicago to fight for the title. I'll face the most fearsome wolves from all over the continent. You know what that means, right?"

My insides clench. I can't think about him dying. My life would be over. "Well, maybe someone else could be alpha and--"

"There's no way." He shakes his head, and his long hair tickles my face. "I'll become enemy number one after Thorn is gone. This is why I've been so slow to do anything about him. I wasn't ready to put myself or my pack in that kind of danger. I can see now that I was a coward."

"I don't think you're a coward."

"Tell that to all the men and women I've failed." His voice cracks, and there's nothing I can say because he's right. My sister is dead, and my family is lost to me because of his pack and his right-hand man. But maybe when this is all over and Ryne is in charge of things, I'll get to see my parents and little brother again. Maybe everything will change. Ryne had said that he wants to allow the mating to happen by choice--whether it's women married to wolves they love or women being paid to have the children of the pack. Either would be infinitely better than what's happening now.

Ryne freezes.

"Hey, it's okay--"

"Shh," he says, sitting up slowly. "Did you hear that?"

Before I can answer, he's tearing out of the tent, shifting into his wolf as he goes. I jump up too and hurry to throw on some clothes. My heart is pounding in my chest, and my movements feel too slow. I hear the growls before I see them.

Two wolves.

They circle Ryne, and then they pounce.

The noise wakes everyone up, and one of the guards comes running. "We're under attack!"

I want to scream at him that he's too late, but there's no time for that. I need a weapon. I pick up a long stick and hurry over to what's left of the fire, holding it in.

"Please light," I mutter to myself. But it's not lighting, and I don't have time to sit around and wait for it.

"What's that going to do?" Faye appears beside me, her eyes round and hopeful. She probably thinks she's being rescued right now.

"Do you have any better ideas?" I'll admit it's not my brightest, but I don't see anything else that will make a better weapon. I want a sword or a knife.

Faye shakes her head. She has kept to herself the last few weeks and I'm pretty sure Ryne and I are the only ones who know she wants to return to the wolves. She yanks the stick from my hand and runs toward the fighting wolves. The end is glowing red but it's not on fire.

Better than nothing.

"Damn it, Faye!" I scream and run after her. Now I'm weaponless.

Our little band isn't able to turn into our lycan selves right now, but that doesn't mean we can't fight. We're small, but we're mighty--we may be able to overtake them. There are only two. The problem is that we're nearing the new moon, so that means we're weak. The wolves must know that.

Laik points a gun at the fray and starts shooting.

People scream, and I tackle Laik, the gun catapulting out of his hand and landing on the ground. "You could kill someone!"

"That's the point," he growls, throwing me off him. We don't have many firearms. They're hard to come by, even with the panthers supplying our resistance. Everything that's left is from before the wars, and most of it was destroyed.

I scramble for the gun, but Wanda beats me to it. "You want to die today?" She cackles at me, waving the gun in my face. I fully expect her to turn it on me, but she doesn't. She starts shooting at the wolves as well, but lucky for them, she's a terrible shot.

"I'm out of ammo," she whines, throwing it back to Laik.

"Yeah, and you wasted it, woman!"

She laughs and unsheathes a long knife from her belt, running head-on toward the wolves.

Elle is there now. The wolves are fighting two against two.

I look around for Joanna and Grady because we could really use his help right now, but he's nowhere to be seen. I can't believe they're not here helping. Where the hell are they?

A wolf gets his jaw around Ryne, but Ryne tosses him off, so he goes for Elle instead. She cries out when it gets her leg. It's a piercing sound that drives right to my center, but I know she'll recover. Wolves heal fast. Ryne goes for the wolf again, ripping him away from Elle and then finishes him.

Blood sprays, and the body goes limp.

The final wolf backs off with a growl but drops to its hind legs and starts to whimper.

Elle changes back to her human form, rubbing her bloodied leg. "Justin, what are you doing here?" she yells at the wolf.

I gasp. I hadn't recognized his wolf in the fray. Faye stands to my left, her burning stick hanging limp in her hands. She drops it, moving forward. Ryne stands over him, still in his wolf form as well.

Justin gives a slight shake of his head, turns, and runs

away. Ryne immediately gives chase, with Faye right behind him. Elle stays behind to nurse her leg, and I groan and take off as well. I have no idea what's about to happen, but I can't let Faye get hurt, and I worry that this might be a trap for Ryne.

I've always been a good runner, and since being in the wilds, I've gotten better at dodging trees and avoiding roots. Faye runs faster than I expect, but I still overtake her. I don't stop to bother with her though. I just want to make sure that Ryne is safe.

I keep my senses tuned to the padding of his footfalls and the rustle of leaves. I'm falling behind because I can't run as fast as the wolves, but I can't give up.

All at once they stop, and I continue in the direction I last heard them. There's a clearing up ahead, and I really, really hope this isn't some trap where the wolves have Ryne cornered. I don't think I could fight them.

My saliva is useless in the middle of the month.

Just before I reach the edge of the woods, a body hits me from the side, and I go flying. I hit the ground with a thud, and for a second I see stars. A hand covers my mouth, and I jerk my head back and forth.

My vision clears.

Ryne straddles me, his eyes wide with fright.

I still, and he removes his hand, climbing off of me. He's completely naked, but I'm so used to his body by now that it doesn't faze me. He offers to help me stand, and I take it. I rise to my tiptoes and kiss him on the cheek. "Faye's right behind me," I whisper low in his ear.

He shakes his head. "She lost the trail and ran in a different direction. Elle's going after her."

"How do you know?" I ask.

He points to his head. I'd forgotten about the telepathic link, and I definitely want to know what Justin said to him, but now is not the time.

"What's going on?" I ask.

He takes my hand and leads me to the edge of the clearing. I peer through the bushes and leaves. It's another lycan camp but much bigger than ours. Several large men--lycan--patrol the area, all carrying massive guns. How did they get them? Laik acts like the few guns we have are made of gold. In the middle of the camp is a large group of people, all tied up and gagged. They look tired and beaten down. One tries to get up, but the man patrolling the area closest to him kicks him back.

Tents are set up on the far side. This looks like one of the military camps I'd seen in a book once. They're nothing like our tents.

"What is this?" I ask, keeping my voice down. "This isn't our resistance, is it?"

Ryne shakes his head. "I have no idea. But take a good sniff. Are any of them human?"

I let my senses take over. I don't smell human anywhere, just lycan.

"Why would they tie up their own kind?"

"Your guess is as good as mine, but come on, we need to get out of here before we get caught."

We retreat slowly so we don't make enough noise to attract their attention. Once I'm sure we are out of earshot, I grab Ryne's hand and pull him close to me. "I was so scared they were going to hurt you."

He chuckles. "You have little faith in my abilities."

"I have a lot of faith in your abilities, but two attacked at once, and even you aren't invincible."

He kisses my forehead. "I know."

"Did Justin say anything to you?"

"He did. Thorn wants me back, dead or alive. Justin volunteered to be on the search party. The other wolf was one of Thorn's lackeys, and Justin thinks he would've killed me if he'd gotten the chance. That right there tells you a lot about my father."

"I'm so sorry." I don't know what else to say. This isn't good.

"Justin says he and the rest of the betas are still loyal to me, but they are pretending not to be in order to keep Thorn happy." He swallows hard. "As long as I'm still alive, I'm still their alpha. Not even my father can change that."

"And what's been reported of Anders is true?"

"Justin confirmed things have gotten bad with Anders and I'm pretty sure he'll try to kill me when I go back. My betas no longer trust him, not that they ever did."

"I'm sorry."

He shrugs. "The good news is we won't have to fight alone."

"That is good news."

He tightens his hold on my hand. "The full moon will be here soon. We need a plan, and now, after seeing Justin, I think I have a good one."

CHAPTER 30

We get back to camp before I can ask Ryne to explain his plan in full, and Faye is already there, pacing like a caged tiger. She rushes up to me and drags me away from everyone.

"Where the hell is Justin?" she asks. Her hair is a mess of red around her face, and her eyes are rimmed with tears.

I hate that I'm the one to tell her this. "He's on his way back to the city."

"Why didn't you make sure he took me with him?" she hisses.

I rub my forehead. I knew Faye was going to be a problem. "Look, Justin was here trying to warn Ryne. It wasn't a good situation. I'll get you back to him, but it wouldn't have worked for us to send you now. How would you explain your sudden reappearance without having to explain about where you've been?"

"I would've lied, you idiot."

"Or you would've gotten us all killed. I'll make sure that

no matter what we decide to do on the full moon, you'll be in my group. I'll get you as close to Justin's house as I can, and you can slip away.

She chews on her bottom lip, as if thinking, and then nods. "That's a good idea. His mom likes me. She'll take me in until we can figure out the next step."

I'm actually pretty surprised at that. Faye isn't exactly a sweet girl, but maybe she knows how to make it look like she is. Or is it possible she's changed?

"But if that doesn't work, your secret is out," she adds. Guess that answers that.

I gaze past her to where Ryne is arguing with Laik. The two look like they are about to come to blows, but before they do, several people enter the camp, including Madame Delphine. The fact that she traveled this far is astonishing and incredibly dangerous, but I'm too happy to see her to think about that much.

I leave Faye and rush up to her, crushing her in a hug. The woman is a motherly figure to me, and I just want her to know how much I appreciate her. She doesn't react at first, but slowly her arms come around me and tighten. Something loosens in my chest, an unburdening I've been needing. I don't know how long we stand there, but it's long enough that I start to miss my family, my father especially, and I'm no longer unburdened.

She pulls away and just looks at me without a word. Then she squeezes my hand and steps around me to give Ryne a hug.

Laik clears his throat. "What are you doing here?"

She glances over at him. "We have a monster to kill, don't we? We need a plan. We've done a decent job of rescuing some women, but we need to change the course of history if we're going to save them all."

Ryne stands a little taller. "And I know exactly how we are going to do that."

"It's a bad idea," Laik growls.

Ryne clenches his fists. "It's not. You've proven that the lycan are unpredictable. If I use my men to stage an uprising, we can kill Thorn without the risk of too many people dying."

"What are you talking about?" I ask. If Ryne's planning on leaving the lycan behind, it means he'll leave me behind as well, and I can't have that.

He turns to me. "I want to take Thorn out using the betas. If I can get Justin and my most trusted men to back me up, we can ambush my father. The festival won't be about taking girls to the mating house. It will be my return as the alpha and ending my father's tyranny. There will be a fight, but I think most of the wolves will back me up. Once Thorn is dead, we'll take out any wolves who aren't on our side and head to Chicago as a group, gathering allies along the way."

It's actually a really good plan, but Laik is glaring at him, and Madame Delphine frowns.

"You're completely leaving out the lycan," Laik scoffs.

"I'm asking that you not be involved until after I've killed Thorn and established myself as King Alpha. I don't want you in my city, but you can come with us to Chicago as our backup."

"That's the thing, Ryne. You aren't going to be the King Alpha," Madame Delphine says in a soft voice.

"Why the hell not?"

"Because the Resistance has already had a plan in place for a long time. Izaak will take over as the king, and you will remain here presiding over the Carolina Pack."

"Who's Izaak?" Laik questions.

"Elle's father. He's high up in the Resistance movement."

This is all news to me. I try to recall what I know of Elle's father, but nothing is coming to me besides what I saw of him at the last festival. He seemed like a formidable man with a strong no-nonsense type of way about him and a soft spot for his family. Elle certainly loves him, but can we trust her to be able to see past the blind spots when it comes to her own father? What if he's no better than the rest of them? Elle is still off in the woods so she isn't here right now to weigh in, but I wonder how much she knows about all this. Probably a lot more than she's let on.

"Why Izaak?" Ryne asks, his brow furrowed. "Wouldn't that cause more unrest? He's been rivals with Thorn for years. Someone new would be better."

"I'm sorry, but this plan has been in place for far longer than you have been the alpha of the Carolina Pack." It feels like a wall has gone up between mother and son, and my heart aches for them both. "We didn't know if you would be for or against your father."

"And your husband."

"He's not my husband anymore, but he will always be your father." She clears her throat and steps back. "We have to let things go on as planned. Too many people are counting on it. I do like the idea of you taking Thorn out with the help of your betas, but then you need to bring the lycan in for damage control."

"My men will never go for that," Ryne argues.

"Neither will mine," Laik says. "We're nobody's damage control."

Madame Delphine shakes her head, frustration painting her cheeks red. She points at them as she speaks. "And you two wonder why the Resistance waits until the last minute to bring you in on our plans. I don't care if you like it or not. If we are going to change the world and save women from the fate that currently exists for them, you will do as I say."

It's almost humorous watching both men stare down Madame Delphine. I know from experience how intimidating she can be. And quite frankly, she's not just talking about our city. She's talking about cities all over that need liberation. She's thinking big here, and that starts with the lycans and wolves cooperating with each other.

"I want to be the Alpha King," Ryne pushes again. "I can do far more good than Izaak. You know that. He's a fine man, but he's too wrapped up in politics and has almost as many enemies as Thorn."

"And you don't have enemies?" Laik snorts.

"Not many." Ryne glares between Laik and his mother. "My vision for the future is a fair one that I cannot enact unless I'm the one in charge."

Some may say he sounds selfish, but to me he sounds like the alpha I know him to be. Leadership runs in his veins, and he's been stomped down too many times to keep taking it.

"Ryne, can we argue about this another day? We have precious little time to make sure that we have a solid plan for the festival." Delphine gives him a pointed look.

Ryne jams his hand in his hair. "The plan will change because I'm the one going to Chicago."

"Please don't make this difficult. We can't afford to squabble among ourselves right now."

Ryne clenches and unclenches his fists, his face contorted. He's seething mad, but there's something more. There's betrayal. His own mother doesn't believe in him, and it makes me want to riot with him. "Fine," he says at last. "But this conversation is not over."

I'm so torn on what I want to happen. Part of me wants to support Ryne in this, but the other part of me really hopes he doesn't get his way. Because if he does, there's a real possibility he could die before he ever makes it to Chicago.

CHAPTER 31

I can feel the moon like I breathe air. I don't have to think about it--it's automatic. She grows stronger a little more each night, and so do I. We spend the time before she's full again getting everything ready for her. It's going to take the entire Resistance working together to pull this off, but it's possible. We're not just taking down Thorn. We're dismantling an entire system: a system that a lot of wolves still support.

Ryne and I decide not to confront Laik about the other lycan we saw because we're pretty sure they're not with the Resistance. There are other groups out here in the wilds, and they're not our primary concern right now. Tensions are already too high, and we need to focus on staying ahead of our enemies while building an unbreakable plan of attack.

We get together with different Resistance members several times over the following days to go over everything–weighing our options and discussing all the possible outcomes. Every last variable is accounted for––at least we hope so. Nobody's sure if Ryne's plan to use his betas is going to work, but it's the best one we've got.

Regardless, I believe in Ryne.

He wants this. I can see it in his eyes. That want is stronger than anything I've seen in him before, maybe even stronger than the love I see when he looks at me. Because that man is living with painful regrets, and this is his way to make things right again. Or at least, as close to right as he can. The damage has been done. We all know that. Nobody can fix what has happened, just like nobody can bring the dead back to life.

But someone has to make it stop.

On the day of the full moon, we split up into several groups. We're entering the city from three different points, just in case someone gets caught. The other lycan groups that are partnered with the Resistance have joined us, plus some of the lone wolves like Grady. There are far more of us than I thought. There's at least two hundred in all.

"I wish we had panthers to help us too," I say to Charlotte. She's with me, Ryne, Knox, Faye, and a few others. Joanna, Grady, and Callum are with a different group.

"That would solidify our win, wouldn't it?" She sighs. "I still don't understand why they aren't here, considering this is their battle too."

"They can't risk it," Ryne points out. "It would be seen as an act of war, and they're more inclined to hide behind the lycans now, aren't they?" He's been conflicted about them in the past, but he now thinks they're cowards for skirting around the treaty. I can't say I blame him. "We don't need them anyway."

Knox rolls his eyes and takes a long swig from his canteen. "Whatever you say, boss."

There's a friction between the two men that's grown by the day. I can't quite put my finger on it exactly, but I can sense it's there.

"We're getting closer," Wanda says. "Time to shut your traps."

I glare at her back as she continues to lead us down the forest path. I don't like Laik, but I really don't like Wanda. At this point, I'd take him leading us over her, but he's coming in from a different direction. It's all part of the plan. We have to split up our strongest fighters, just in case. We can't have any weak links.

For the next hour, everyone stays quiet. There are wolves patrolling the area, watching for us. I thank my lucky stars, yet again, that my lycan DNA makes it hard for them to sense or track me, but having Faye and Ryne with us is a big liability. We have to be extra careful.

I also thank my lucky stars that we're not crossing the bridge again--that was given to Joanna's group. No, we're coming in one of the back ways, similar to how Knox and I left the city in the first place. There's an old highway nearby that's been broken into pieces, and every once in a while, we can see it through the trees.

When we pass by one of the villages, I find myself looking at it a little too long. It's not my home, and my family isn't there, but I can imagine they are. I can see myself climbing the trees and working in the fields. Hiding out indoors during the full moons, expecting the wolf shifters to protect me from the evil lycan.

My eyes fill with hot tears. If they could see me now, I don't even know if my family would want anything to do with me. Maybe Papa. Probably Evan. But definitely not Mama. She was never one to step outside the lines, and associating with a lycan would be out of the question.

The tears fall, and Ryne squeezes my hand. He doesn't ask if I'm okay—he knows I'm not. And he doesn't ask me why I'm crying. Being fated to him is similar to being beholden to the moon. I couldn't stop it if I tried. It's who I am now.

Wanda picks up the pace, and nobody complains. The sun has just set, and the moon is still behind the horizon, but it won't be much longer. Once that light peeks over the horizon we're goners. It grows darker, and we start to run. It doesn't matter if we're monsters when we enter the city, but the farther we can get away from the villages, the better.

"Are you sure you want to do this?" Ryne whispers to me one last time. He's asked it before, and I've done the same. I don't respond because he already knows my answer.

There's no turning back now.

We come to the first house and stop in a cropping of nearby trees. "This is it," Wanda says. "Don't let the Resistance down, or I'll kill you myself."

"Gee--nice pep talk." I roll my eyes.

I know this house on the outskirts of the city. It's Justin's family home, located on the river. They have a pontoon waiting for us on their dock. We run to it and climb aboard, staying silent as Ryne starts the engine. This will get us downtown the fastest, and we need to be fast if we're going to get into position before the moon rises.

At the last second, Faye jumps off the boat and sprints for the house.

"What are you doing?" Wanda hisses after her.

"It's okay." I hold up my hands. "Let her go. She never wanted to fight. She just used us to get back to her beta wolf."

I can tell Wanda wants to tear after her and pull her back by her hair, but we're running out of time. Faye disappears around the corner of the house and is quickly forgotten. We have way more important things to worry about than her.

As if reading my thoughts, Ryne looks up toward the starry sky where a faint light is hovering near the horizon, and he winces. "I'm going to use the highest speed. Everybody hang on."

We start by bouncing across the waves to soon flying across them. It's going to draw attention to our boat, but hopefully not too much. The Buck Moon Festival is tonight, and the July heat will linger all night long. My skin is sticky from it, but also from my lycan--she's ready to be released. I can feel her digging at my muscles and heating my blood.

When we get to the dock, two guards come running.

"Prince Ryne?" One of them lets out a gasp. "You're back?"

The other gives our party a curious glance, his lip curling when he catches our scent.

"You will speak of this to no one," Ryne says hastily.

"I'm still your alpha, and you cannot defy me."

"But--"

"Unless you wish to fight for my title right now?" He raises an eyebrow. "I'll admit a delta has never been alpha before, but there is a first for everything."

"I would never," one says as the other shakes his head. Then they bow to their alpha.

"Now tell me if the festival has started," Ryne says, and they nod. "Is my father there yet?" They nod again.

"You both stay and watch this boat. Make sure nobody takes it," he instructs them. They don't argue in the slightest as we scramble from the boat and up the dock, leaving them behind.

Wanda's eyes are wide and angry, but she doesn't say anything. Knox and Charlotte exchange an unreadable glance, and the other two lycan stare at the alpha wolf with newfound interest--probably because Laik doesn't have this kind of power even though he claims to be their alpha. It's clear to me now that he's taken his power by force and nothing else. He makes people pledge loyalty to him, but it's only words. He must hate that the wolves have something he'll never have.

Our group is supposed to wait nearby until Ryne gives the signal that it's time to move. I don't like waiting on the sidelines and want to go in there to kill Thorn myself, but I've never taken a life, and I'm not sure I would have the guts to do it. It's better if Ryne does it. His pack needs to see he's still the one in power. We'll come in as reinforcements.

This will change everything.

The other groups are assembling outside the festival as

well, but at different vantage points. Madame Delphine and Elle are going to sever the phone lines to the city and plan to take off the moment Thorn is dead. They have to go to Chicago to deliver the news and make sure Izaak takes the throne. All of the packs under Thorn's rule will feel the moment he is dead, but they won't know what happened or why. Brawls will break out, but it's important to the Resistance that Elle's father is the one to gain favor and become the ruling family. Anyone else, and we could be in an even worse situation than we already are. Deep down, I fear it won't be that easy. If Ryne is right, and Izaak has a lot of enemies, then he'll face challenges not only to take the throne, but to keep it.

If things don't work out, Ryne is fully prepared to go to Chicago. He hasn't told me as much, but I know him, and I know he will do what needs to be done.

The festival is happening in the same park where the spring one took place. There are no weddings this time, but there is dancing underway. The lively orchestra music filters through the trees as we get into position.

Ryne gives me a tight hug and whispers in my ear. "No matter what, I want you to stick to the plan."

I don't agree or say anything. He should know me better than that. This plan isn't perfect, and neither are the people implementing it, so if need be, I'll throw it all aside like a scrap of paper. He's the same, and maybe that's why fate put us together. He presses a kiss to the top of my head, squeezes my hand, and then he's gone, dashing through the trees.

"Do you feel that?" Wanda sighs blissfully. "It's almost time for our renewal."

I find the best shadow I can and strip down to my underwear. I doubt I'll still be in the city when the moon sets tomorrow morning, but just in case, I want to have clothing and shoes somewhere waiting for me. I'm still not used to all this nudity and doubt I ever will be.

Just as I finish undressing, the moon makes her appearance, and my bones crack.

CHAPTER 32

I stand taller and broader in this form, and my senses come alive with pristine clarity. My thoughts are my own. It's better than it was last time and completely different than it was on my first renewal. I still feel like myself. And what's more--I don't feel like a monster. I feel like a goddess. I'm powerful and free and amazing.

I like it.

The park is huge, and the festival is taking place in the center. We're in a cluster of trees for cover, but that's all. There's not much to keep us from being discovered, and I'm sure this place is crawling with guards, not to mention all the wolves here to attend the festival.

One wrong move, and it's over before it even starts.

I look to the others, thankful that we're all keeping still in our new forms, waiting. It's not easy to wait when we're like this, and it's only Knox's second renewal, but he seems to be holding up okay.

I stay the shadows and wait for Ryne's signal. Once he howls, then we'll howl back and descend on the party. But what if Ryne never howls? I tell myself to be patient, but time crawls by slowly, and I'm antsy for action. I feel like something should've happened by now. What if he needs my help?

I can't wait.

I can't get a good enough view of the festival, and I don't like it, so I dig my claws into the thickest tree of the group and climb. The others follow my lead, which wasn't my intention. I tell the lycans nearest me to stop through our telepathic link, but they ignore me, and I can't exactly make them do anything.

Before I know it, I'm in the tops of the trees with the others below me, all scrambling to get a better view, but I forget them and watch the scene on the stage. It's still hard to see, but I know it must be Ryne in a heated battle with his father. Snarls and thumps sound regularly over the orchestra music, but the view is obscured by the beta wolves who are crowding. Someone screams, and the music stops. It takes a minute for people to realize what's going on, but once they do, they're quick to run toward the stage.

Suddenly, a wolf goes flying out of the middle of the crowd and lands with a thud on the grass. Nobody moves to help and they all back away. There's a ripple of confusion in the crowd. A few of them shift. I squint, and a calm understanding washes through me at the same time as complete horror. It's Ryne--he's not moving.

My heart plummets.

I leap from the tree, landing hard on my feet, but it

doesn't hurt. A few men around me cry out, but I ignore them and rush for Ryne, praying that he's not dead. I reach him at the same time that a giant black wolf with a white stripe across his nose lands near him. He snarls and leaps for Ryne, his jaws open, going for the neck. I've seen this move too many times before. If he reaches Ryne, he'll tear his throat right out.

I rush in front of Ryne, my own jaws snapping. Thorn crushes me on top of Ryne, and I flail, not knowing which end is up. My jaws connect with flesh above me, and I clamp down, hoping that my venom will kill Thorn. All at once, I'm thrown in the air and land on my stomach as my face snaps down on the ground, causing stars to flash behind my eyes.

I shake my head and crawl onto all fours. Ryne still lies on the ground, blood pouring from various wounds. Thorn stands over him, about to go in for the kill. He's determined, and nothing will stop him, not even a lycan. A sword glints on the ground, and I don't know how it got there, but I don't hesitate.

I grab the sword in my clawed hands and rush for Thorn. We trained hard with swords at Drayton Hall, and I remember my lessons on using solid footing. It's different being in this form, but it's still familiar enough that I know what to do. I raise the sword over my head, but before I can bring it down, someone collides with me from the side. We both hit the stage, and the sword clatters out of my hand.

The wolf snaps his jaws at me, and I growl. I only need to get one bite in to sign his death warrant. It won't kill him instantly, but it will slow him down enough that I can finish the job. But he's good. He manages to avoid my teeth. Out of the corner of my eye, I glimpse the sword just beyond my reach. I wiggle to the side and lurch over like I'm going to bite his paw, and the distraction is enough for me to grab the sword. I snatch it up and drive it right into the wolf's heart.

He goes limp, and I shove him off of me, leaping back up.

Ryne has gotten to his feet and is fighting with Thorn again, but he's weak and is losing badly. They're in their wolf forms, but I know exactly what I'm seeing, a father and son fighting to the death. My heart shatters. Ryne never should've had to do this. It's not fair, and now he's going to die at his father's hands.

No.

I won't let that happen. I can't.

I rush toward them, raise my sword, and arc it toward Thorn's neck. It slices hard, and hot blood spurts in all directions. His wolf body crumples to the ground, his snarling head landing a few paces away. I don't think I can cry in this form, but if I was my normal self, I know I'd be sobbing.

Ryne collapses on the other side of his father's corpse, and I rush for him. There is a huge bite on his flank, blood matted with fur, and horror sets in when I realize that it's a lycan bite.

My lycan bite. I didn't bite Thorn as intended.

I bit Ryne.

CHAPTER 33

He's not dead yet. He's not dead yet. He's not dead yet.

It's a mantra that rings through my mind as I watch Ryne, while breaking into a million razor-edged pieces. Lycan venom takes time to kill a wolf--two or three days. But it's not Ryne's only wound, and the pain he's going to experience will undo us both. The compassionate thing to do would be to end his life now, to spare him from his fate. But I can't. I release my own howl--an ugly screech that echoes into the night. My insides feel hollow. I know I've killed Thorn, but when Ryne dies, I'll be alone.

I gather up his wolf body and run into the frenzied crowd. The other lycans have descended, and the world is in pure chaos. I don't care about any of that though. I only want to spend time with Ryne away from everyone else before he dies. A few wolves fall into step with me, and I automatically growl. But I recognize Justin and Nico, and I swallow hard. Are they going to kill me for this? Do they understand it was an accident? I can't forgive myself, I never will, so I can't expect them to either.

They were loyal to their alpha to the end, and here they are, loyal still. We run together, the three of us with Ryne's limp body in my arms. Pain wells in my chest, but I can't lose it yet. I need to wait until I'm human again. Not as much time has passed as I thought. We still have hours before the moon sets.

The other lycans are wrangling the crowd now. The next part of the plan is in full swing, but I can't think about that right now. All I can think about is Ryne.

He's still alive.

He's still alive, and I'm going to keep him that way as long as I can.

We manage to get out of town without incident and escape into the woods near the village we had passed earlier. It's exhausting, and my lycan body isn't as strong as I expected, but I don't even care. I have to get to privacy. I catch sight of a clearing and run to it, finally letting myself stop.

I carefully lay Ryne on the ground and assess his wounds. It's so hard with my overly large lycan hands and sharp claws. Tears course down my gross snout, and I sit back on my haunches. Everything about me is wrong right now. This isn't *me*!

Justin and Nico both turn back into humans and push me aside. They must know who I am or at least suspect it because they don't seem bothered that I'm here. At least I have that. I'm grateful they don't act as if they're going to hurt me because I couldn't stand to fight one of them.

"I'm going to run into the village and see if they have

bandages," Nico says. I nod since I can't respond, and he takes off, shifting into his wolf as he goes.

Justin just stares at Ryne. "You know, we really should just put him out of his misery."

I shake my head fiercely.

"Poppy. He's going to die slowly and painfully. You really want him to suffer?"

I don't respond. I don't want to accept that Ryne's going to die. He can't. Not yet.

Justin looks around and grabs a large stick. "Fine, if you won't do it, then I will." He raises it high over his head.

I howl and throw myself over Ryne. Justin just glares at me, but I don't move. I won't let him hurt my mate. Maybe I'm selfish, or maybe I'm foolish, but I can't accept that this is the end. Ryne can't die. He just can't.

Ryne whimpers and twists, and then he shifts back into his human body. He's naked and vulnerable, but it allows me to get a better look at his wounds. They're worse than I thought. The angry bite mark on his torso festers, and he clutches at it but doesn't regain consciousness. I stay where I am, fully prepared to fight Justin off if I must.

A few minutes later, Nico jogs up empty-handed. "Poppy, you have to see this."

I want to ask what "this" is, but of course I can't. I can't even argue with him. I gather Ryne back up in my arms. I would never be able to do this as a human, but as a lycan it's easy. It would also be easy to end his pain. It would be as quick as a kiss.

"Leave him with Justin. We'll be back in a second," Nico says.

I give a fierce shake of my head. Nico looks between me

and Justin, who has stayed strangely quiet. I long to tell Nico what Justin attempted to do while he was gone, but of course I can't. Nico is smart though. He assesses Justin with a scowl but doesn't address it.

"Fine. Follow me," he says, motioning for us to get up.

I lift Ryne again, and this time his eyes open, and he blinks rapidly. "Poppy?" His voice is scratchy with anguish. "Poppy--" He coughs, blood splatters down his chest, and then he passes out again.

"Once he's dead, the alpha bond will break, and the betas will begin to fight over our pack," Justin says to Nico. "Your father will likely win the spot. Are you sure you don't want to go back for that?"

Nico laughs bitterly. "I'd rather not see that, but thanks." He nods toward the direction he came from. "Now, come on before they're gone."

I'm curious who he's talking about. Tucking Ryne closer to my body and ducking under the low-hanging branches, I follow him as quietly as I can. He and Justin shift back into their wolves and slip through the forest like water through a brook. It's so natural and easy for them. I soon find that it's the same way for me, despite Ryne's dripping blood that tickles my senses. The moon's power is stronger than anything I've felt before.

That's not true.

I've felt grief much stronger than this.

And heartache. I'm feeling that now.

And a little bit of denial.

After a few minutes, we come upon the water's edge and duck into the tall grass to watch. There's a large boat, with lycan standing on the shore. The moonlight seems to favor them compared to the humans they're with.

Wait, why are they with humans?

This was never part of the plan. Then again, I don't recognize any of the lycan. Several of the humans are already on the boat, crying. Another lycan approaches, dragging two humans with him. They're women I don't recognize. Could they be saving them from the mating houses?

They must be.

I start to relax, and then the lycan bears down on the women and bites them both in quick succession. They scream, and my world flips upside down.

CHAPTER 34

I have to stop them. But I'm holding Ryne, and he's losing blood quickly. Do I save these women? Can I save them? It might be too late, but I can't just watch and do nothing. before I can make my decision, the last of them are on the boat, and they're moving out. We sink back into the shadows. The wolves growl, as do I. In this, we're together.

I want to kill those lycan. They took the choice from those women. It wasn't an accident. It was planned. How long has this been going on? A memory surfaces--the other group of lycan Ryne and I saw in the woods a few weeks ago. They'd had several lycan with them who were tied up. They smelled like lycan to me at the time, but maybe they were humans who were on their way to their first renewal? They could have easily been people who'd been bitten on the previous full moon. I know what it's like to feel your life draining slowly away between full moons.

Imagine having to go through that knowing your bite wasn't an accident but was intentional.

I look to the wolves and hold Ryne up to them. They nod in understanding. We have to tend to Ryne's wounds before we can do anything else. He can't travel much farther, so I move away from the shoreline to a quiet place in the trees and sit with him while they go. I don't know how long it takes for them to get medical supplies because I get lost looking at the man I love--the man I've sentenced to an early and horrific death.

I can't say goodbye to him. Not yet. Not like this while I'm still trapped in this monster's body.

They return, wearing clothes and carrying supplies. Faye is with them, holding hands with Justin. I guess she wasn't lying after all. She gives me a little wave and a sad smile. The men kneel before us and get to work patching Ryne's wounds. Normally he'd have healed on his own by now, but the lycan venom must be slowing down that process.

He cries out in his sleep when they stitch him up, the shiny needle and black thread piercing through his skin like claws. Then they apply ointment and wrap bandages around the rest of the wounds.

"Where to?" Nico asks, and Justin raises his eyebrow. "What? I'm not leaving my alpha until I have to."

"Same," Justin says grimly.

So I pick Ryne up, and together the five of us head toward the lycan camp. It's going to take a few hours of walking, and I have no idea what to expect when I get there, but I can't imagine things could get any worse than they already have.

The camp is in disarray when we arrive just after the moon sets. I hand Ryne off to Justin and Nico right before my body transitions to its human form. Normally I'd be happy about that, but I can't think about anything except Ryne right now. I hurry and slip into some clothing and go looking for help, the two men follow close behind.

Our plan didn't go as we'd hoped, considering Ryne's state, but at least Thorn is dead. I've never killed before, and I never want to do it again, but part of me is glad I was the one to do it. Ryne never should've had to kill his own father, And I'd do anything to save Ryne.

I shake my head, angry at myself for the thought. I didn't save Ryne. That's the last thing I did. I'll never forgive myself for my mistake. I ignore all the craziness in camp and find the medic tent still set up.

We slip in, and the guys set Ryne down on a cot. I cover him up with a blanket and smooth his hair back from his face. A body slumps down next to mine.

"What happened to him?" Callum asks. He gives Nico and Justin a skeptical look, his nostrils flaring.

"I bit him by accident." I cringe and look away.

Callum puts an arm around my shoulder. "I'm so sorry. Is there anything I can do?"

I wipe the tears that dot my face. "I know it's supposed to be painful. Can you give him something?"

"Yeah, let me see what I can find."

"You should put him out of his misery," Justin says again, sinking onto the cot across from us.

I shake my head fiercely. "No. What if you're wrong, and the venom doesn't actually kill him?"

"It will. No one has ever survived."

"Maybe. But you usually kill them before they even have a fighting chance, don't you?" They don't answer. "Well, I'm going to give him that chance."

"Fine," he grinds out. "But don't come crying to me when he's in so much pain you can't stand watching it."

I can feel Justin's anger, and I know it's deeper than that. He's heartbroken too. Nico still doesn't speak. His eyes are closed, and he's frozen in place, as if he's trying to imagine he's anywhere but here.

The tent flap opens, and several more people enter. I don't even bother to look up. I only have eyes for Ryne.

"What the hell did you do?" Laik booms and I jump. He grabs me by my hair and pulls me from the tent, throwing me to the dirt. Everyone surrounds us, but Nico and Justin stay by the tent door, protecting the entrance to Ryne.

I jump up and spin on Laik. "I killed Thorn. Wasn't that the plan?"

He jams his hand through his filthy hair. "No. The plan was for Ryne to kill Thorn and take control over his pack again. Do you realize what a mess you made back there?"

"But Ryne--"

"And now we have to leave the territory because there's no telling who will win the battles for alpha and what they will do. Ryne was more interested in protecting his soldiers than trying to hunt us down out here. How do we know the next son of a bitch won't be?" He shakes his head violently. "I'm certain that there's going to be an extensive manhunt to find whoever killed the Alpha King."

"But Ryne's not dead yet. No one should be taking over for his pack."

Laik glares at me. "They know he's on his way. They

saw the bite, Poppy! We had to retreat because Anders all but incited a riot."

I glance at Justin and Nico. "You two should go back. Fight for your alpha."

Justin shakes his head. "Nope. You decided to keep him alive. I'm staying with him until he dies."

"Me too," Nico says. "And besides, I'm happy being a beta. I don't want to be an alpha, and I won't fight my father to get it."

I take in the rest of the crowd. Faye sits down. Charlotte and Knox hover behind her. Joanna and Grady stand near the entrance of the tent. There's a funny look on Grady's face--like he's both heartbroken and relieved at the same time.

"Kill him now. We have to move, and we can't be slowed down by a dying wolf," Laik says.

I stand and face Laik. "I'm sorry, who put you in charge? I don't remember swearing allegiance to you, and you're not a real alpha."

"What did you just say to me?"

"You're not! Lycan don't have pack bonds like the wolves do. There's a difference between loyalty and blood, and you know it."

He takes a long breath, a blood vessel popping along his sweaty forehead. "Delphine and Elle are headed up to Chicago to smooth things over and to make sure Elle's father takes control as the King Alpha. That leaves me as the leader of the Resistance down here."

"Wouldn't that be Derek?" I scoff, thinking of the intelligent panther who would be a far better leader than Laik.

It's too bad the panthers didn't join us because it could've changed things for the better.

"Do you see that spineless panther anywhere?" Laik shouts in my face, and I rear back. He thinks he's the leader now, huh? Rage rises in my chest as I remember what the lycan were doing on the banks of the river.

"Okay. Leader. Explain the fact that several lycan were turning humans against their will tonight."

Laik's face is smooth and expressionless. "What are you talking about?" he asks, but there's obvious deciet in his tone, and I want to slap him for them.

Wanda cackles. "She's no dummy, that one. You've discovered our master plan."

"Shut up, Wanda," he spits out, and she clams up.

"What's your master plan?" I ask. No one around me seems confused. Callum drops his head, and several others back up.

Laik sighs. "The only way we can defeat the wolves is with an army. Humans are useless."

"Humans are useless?" I gasp. "Their freedom is what you're fighting for!"

"In the future, sure. But right now, humans are either collateral damage, or they're weapons. Which would you rather have in a war?"

The realization of what he's saying hits me hard. "So you're forcing them to become lycan? How is that any better than the mating houses?" My eyes water, and my fists clench. I want to kill him for this.

"At least then they can defend themselves," Charlotte says with a shrug. "Being a lycan isn't so bad. I'd rather be a lycan than stuck in my old life."

I glare at her. "You agree with him?"

"The wolves need to be annihilated, Poppy. Surely you see that?" Knox says. He straightens next to her and puts an arm around her shoulders.

Justin and Nico have gone stony still, but they're staring at the lycans with as much hatred in their eyes as I currently feel. This is evil. Pure evil.

I shake my head. "Absolutely not. The point of the Resistance is to take out the bad wolves, not the entire race."

"Well, that's our plan." Laik rolls his eyes as if he's talking to a naïve child. "I'm sorry if you don't like it. The wolves who join us will be spared, but none of the rest. We need to move. If you don't kill Ryne this instant, I will."

"You can't!"

"You're not thinking clearly." He sneers. "I know what you are. I've known what you were since the day I brought you back here." He swings his arms wide and looks at the others. "Don't listen to her. She'll never be fair when it comes to that dog. She's his fated mate!"

CHAPTER 35

I hurry to the entrance of the tent to stand with Justin and Nico. Justin shifts to his wolf form and growls, and Nico takes on a fighter's stance. "You will not touch him," he spits.

Laik laughs, but he shouldn't. He's no longer a lycan, and these men could rip him to shreds.

"So you've known all this time about me and Ryne, and you said nothing?" I give him a glare.

"I was waiting for the perfect timing. Are you really so dumb that you'd think none of us knew about your stunt at the last festival? I gave you so many chances, Poppy. I should've known you were never going to be reasonable until someone manned up and killed your mate." Laik's followers nod their heads as if he's making perfect sense.

"No matter what happens to Ryne, I will never follow you," I say slowly, enunciating every word. "I refuse to buy into a plan where you force people to do something against their will, no matter how noble you think it is. What you are doing is sick and wrong."

Laik closes his eyes. "Fine. You and your little wolf buddies can stay here and fight off the Carolina Pack on your own. We're moving out." He points at me, his finger jabbing into my sternum. I stand tall, not giving even an inch. "You are no longer part of the Resistance."

"That's not your choice to make." I glare. "In fact, I could say the same to you."

Laik snorts. "You're not in charge of anything."

"I am now. Madame Delphine and Elle left for Chicago and I'm guessing they don't know about your plans or what you've been doing behind the scenes, do they?"

His lips curl into a predatory smile. "They don't need to know everything."

It takes all my self-control not to scream. "The Resistance is not about what you're doing. We are about saving people from slavery, not putting them right into another form."

"Poppy's right," Nico says. "We will follow her and not you." Justin pads his feet in the dirt and bares his teeth.

"Me too." Callum surprises everyone, moving to stand next to Nico.

Laik begins to pace in front of us, breathing hard for a few minutes. "Fine. You pathetic lot can stay here and nurse your pitiful wolf. But if you don't come with us now, don't bother searching for us later. We will kill you."

He turns and storms away, Wanda following closely behind him. Knox and Charlotte give me one last look, and then they go too. My heart hurts a little to watch them walk away, but I find I'm not all that surprised.

Grady and Joanna approach us. "Why won't you kill him?" Grady asks, his voice cracking. "I don't like it, but it's the right thing to do."

"Because I have to believe there is some hope." And maybe I'm foolish to think so. He may have days left or hours. And I'm signing up to watch.

Grady glowers. "I can't do this anymore. I can't sit around and watch this place fall apart. Ryne tried to kill me, and even though I forgive him, it doesn't mean I'm okay with what happened. I'm sorry, Poppy, but we're going with our best chance of survival, and that's with Laik."

"He's a monster." I throw up my hands.

"So is he," Grady says, pointing to Ryne's tent. "So are you. So am I. None of us are innocent anymore, but my job is to keep my mate alive, and I'll do whatever it takes to give Joanna a future."

He turns and slumps away. Joanna stares at me for a long moment, her eyes red and shining with tears. I want to beg her to stay, but I know I can't. She wouldn't leave Grady any more than I'd leave Ryne. She rushes forward and wraps me in a tight hug. As I breathe her in, the dam breaks loose. I finally let myself cry. For her, for me, and for all we've lost.

"Take care of yourself, Poppy," she says shakily. then she turns and runs into the early morning darkness, disappearing into the woods.

I go back to sit with Ryne, staring at him as he sleeps restlessly, and then I look at my companions. They've all joined me, huddled around our dying friend. From the looks on our faces, none of us know what's going to happen.

"We're here because it's the right thing to do," I say, gathering my strength. "Because the one thing we have left in this forsaken world is our freedom to choose, and we're not going to choose the wrong side."

"How do we know what side is right and wrong?" Callum asks. "It seems like they're all wrong if you ask me."

"Because we refuse to take away that choice. Because we believe in freedom and in helping the people who need it most. And that whether you're born a wolf or a human, have become infected like I have, or whatever you are--you shouldn't have to hurt innocent people to get what you want."

They all nod, and it gives me the first spark of true hope that I've felt in a long time.

"So what now, boss?" Faye says, and I just blink at her for several moments. She's being serious. There's no snark, no hatred, no tricks. She means it. She's been quiet and her words shake me out of my misery for the tiniest second.

"You sorta signed yourself up for this," Nico chuckles.

"Right . . ." My voice trails off, and I take a moment to gather my thoughts, looking each of them in the eyes. There are only five of us, plus Ryne, but we're all stronger than we ever could've imagined. And I'm proud of us. "I'll be honest. I don't know what's next, and I don't know how to be a leader. But I've come to realize that the best leaders put others first, and they care about their people." I smile softly. "Believe it or not, I care about all of you, and I'm going to fight for your rights just as hard as I'm going to fight for all the men and women who need our help."

I point to Ryne. "But first, we need to save him." I can tell they want to argue, but they don't. "Listen, maybe it's wishful thinking, but we've got to try." I widen my eyes. "The Carolina Pack needs Ryne, and you know it."

"You're right," Justin says, "but I don't know how you can possibly save him. He's as good as dead."

I shake my head. "I refuse to accept that. And it's not because I'm in denial, and it's not because I love him, which I do. It's because he's the strongest alpha that his pack has ever known. He's still alive despite all he's been through tonight. He's trying--he's fighting--so we have to too."

They give me pitying looks. They don't believe it's possible.

"Okay," Justin gives in. "We'll try."

"We're the Resistance now," I say, taking this small victory and running with it. "Not Laik and his people. Not the panthers. Us. Now it's time we start acting like it." I stand up and brush myself off. We have a lot of work to do and countless people depending on us. "Let's get started."

END OF BOOK THREE

The final book in the New World Shifters series will be released in 2022.

www.ingramcontent.com/pod-product-compliance
Lightning Source LLC
Chambersburg PA
CBHW020335310726
48979CB00015B/2380/J

* 9 7 8 1 9 5 0 0 9 3 3 4 2 *